Praise for
Your Brightest Life

"Jessie has done it again. She's written a delightful guide full to the brim of practical advice for the teen girl who wants to enjoy her life and relationships. It's like an intimate conversation with a friend who knows God's Truth and wants to winsomely invite you into it."

DANNAH GRESH, AUTHOR OF *LIES YOUNG WOMEN BELIEVE*

"What a treasure these tips are for those emerging into womanhood! Honest, FUNNY, and oh so wise. Just when you think you're the only one asking such questions, Jessie meets you full on—in a completely comfortable, non-awkward, and wonderful way. Sneak this book under the covers in your dark moments and watch the lights of life turn on!"

ELISA MORGAN, SPEAKER, AUTHOR OF *YOU ARE NOT ALONE* AND PODCAST HOST OF *GOD HEARS HER*

"Not only is *Your Brightest Life* a rare combination of winsome and wise, Jessie Minassian's own trial-tested character and vibrant life fuel the well-fought wisdom within her words. This book is an invaluable, easy-to-live-out guide for young gals in the everyday areas of their lives—friendships, family dynamics, boys, and more. In the areas we live in but rarely think about, Jessie equips readers to proactively live with intention instead of merely reacting to life as it comes. This book is a gold mine for girls who genuinely desire to live better lives."

MEGAN FATE MARSHMAN, SPEAKER AND AUTHOR OF *RELAXED*

"Jessie's vulnerability, stories, and tips make this a very relatable, practical, and inspiring must-read. *Your Brightest Life* includes a treasure trove of wisdom and insights based on biblical truths that every young woman needs to read and take to heart as they lean into faith, relationships, insecurities, and the many challenges life can bring."

DR. DANNY HUERTA, VICE PRESIDENT OF PARENTING
AND YOUTH AT FOCUS ON THE FAMILY AND AUTHOR
OF *7 TRAITS OF EFFECTIVE PARENTING*

Tessie Minassian

Your
BRIGHTEST
Life

TIPS FOR
NAVIGATING
RELATIONSHIPS,
HEALTH, FAITH,
MINDSET,
AND MORE

ZONDERVAN®

ZONDERVAN

Your Brightest Life
Copyright © 2024 by Jessie Minassian

Published in Grand Rapids, Michigan, by Zondervan. Zondervan is a registered trademark of The Zondervan Corporation, L.L.C., a wholly owned subsidiary of HarperCollins Christian Publishing, Inc.

Requests for information should be addressed to customercare@harpercollins.com.

Zondervan titles may be purchased in bulk for educational, business, fundraising, or sales promotional use. For information, please email SpecialMarkets@Zondervan.com.

ISBN 978-0-310-16599-6 (hardcover)
ISBN 978-0-310-16610-8 (audio)
ISBN 978-0-310-16609-2 (ebook)

Library of Congress Cataloging-in-Publication Data

Names: Minassian, Jessie, author.
Title: Your brightest life: tips for navigating relationships, health, faith, mindset, and more / Jessie Minassian.
Description: Grand Rapids, Michigan: Zondervan, [2024] | Audience: Ages 13 and up | Summary: "Today more than ever, as a young woman you can use an extra dose of optimism to tackle the challenges and complicated situations in your life. Inside Your Brightest Life, Jessie Minassian draws on over twenty years of questions and feedback from teen- and college-aged girls to dive into the topics you care about, presenting honest truths and tested tips from a Christian perspective that help you live a life of purpose, joy, and faith"— Provided by publisher.
Identifiers: LCCN 2024021634 (print) | LCCN 2024021635 (ebook) | ISBN 9780310165996 (hardcover) | ISBN 9780310166092 (ebook) | ISBN 9780310166108 (audio)
Subjects: LCSH: Teenage girls—Religious life. | Christian college students—Religious life. | Christian teenagers,—Religious life. | BISAC: YOUNG ADULT NONFICTION / Inspirational & Personal Growth | YOUNG ADULT NONFICTION / Social Topics / Emotions & Feelings
Classification: LCC BV4551.3 .M57 2024 (print) | LCC BV4551.3 (ebook) | DDC 248.8/33—dc23/eng/20240628
LC record available at https://lccn.loc.gov/2024021634
LC ebook record available at https://lccn.loc.gov/2024021635

Published in association with the literary agency of Wolgemuth & Wilson.

Cover design: Micah Kandros Design
Interior design: Denise Froehlich

Printed in the United States of America

24 25 26 27 28 LBC 5 4 3 2 1

*For Ryan Kailey and
Logan Cassidy.*

*You make this one, wild
life all the brighter.*

Contents

Tips About Friends and Family

Tips About Health and Beauty

Tips About Faith

Tips About Mindset

Tips About Life Skills

Introduction

(Read this first!)

I ate poison oak this morning.

If you live in a climate where *Toxicodendron diversilobum* abounds, you might be wondering what the actual heck is wrong with me. On the other hand, if you're not sure why putting that leaf into my mouth is a big deal, then you've obviously never brushed skin with a plant that has the ability to make grown men cry.

See, the lovely red-green leaves of the Pacific poison oak glisten softly in the sunlight because they're coated with urushiol oil. And if just a pinhead's worth of that sticky resin touches your skin? Get ready for painful, itchy sores to wreck your world. Oh, it gets worse. Since it's super easy to spread the oil before you realize you've touched it, the poison easily jumps to arms, legs, and even—ahem—*sensitive areas*. That's a bad day.

So what would possess me to intentionally put that nasty little plant into my mouth?

Jim. It's Jim's fault.

I live in a peaceful town along Central California's coastline. It's the kind of place people make vacation reels from. There's a cool sea breeze, vineyards nestled between rolling hills, cute little surf shops . . . and enough poison oak to cover a small country. In fact, it surrounds my house. Since I love being outside, I would get kind of freaked out that I might go for a walk, casually brush against it, and spend a month in misery. So one day I asked my neighbor Jim—a man who wears suspenders to hold up his weathered work jeans and has earned that head of graying hair—if he knew how to get rid of it.

"Jim," I said, pointing to one of the *many* clusters in my yard, "how do you yank out a plant that bites back?"

"Oh," he said slowly, rubbing the stubble on his chin. "I used to get poison oak real bad."

"Oh?"

"Yeah. Real bad."

Is that supposed to make me feel better about being surrounded? "But now you, what, got rid of it all?"

"No," he said, as he walked toward some just beyond my deck. "What you got to do"—he plucked a glistening, red-tinged leaf off the branch between calloused fingers—"is eat a bit of it."

Concerned for this decent man's life, I considered snatching the leaf away from him before he could do what he seemed to be considering. But that would give *me* a rash, so I selfishly decided to see how this played out.

With my eyes wide and while mumbling a prayer on his behalf, I witnessed Jim put that godforsaken leaf in his mouth.

"Now, you don't want to start out with a whole leaf," he continued through chews. "Pinch off just a little bit to start and work your way to it."

I had about a million questions, and because I'm a millennial, instead of asking the insane man, I took them all to Google.

Q: *Can you eat poison oak?*

A: Strongly ill-advised.

Q: *Can you build an immunity to Toxicodendron diversilobum?*

A: What kind of idiot would want to try?

Q: *How can I tell if my neighbor is superhuman?*

A: Page not found.

But the question that dogged me for a week straight was: Given the evidence before me, was I brave enough to try?

As I considered this, I mentioned the conversation I had with Jim to another, much younger neighbor.

"Hey," I began, hoping she wouldn't think I was crazy, "have you ever heard of someone building up an immunity to poison oak by, say, eating it?"

Her eyes widened. "Oh my gosh, all the old-timers say that! I have no idea if it works. I honestly don't know anyone our age brave enough to try it!"

We laughed because it was true. We are a generation used to instant answers provided by the constant companions in our pockets. But Siri was no help in this situation. Online information (or lack of it) is only as true or *helpful* as the people creating content behind the screens.

Sometimes you find out the best info from the old-timers.

It took me a few months to get up the courage, but I finally did it. I ate a tiny piece of poison oak. Well, I technically *drank* it in a glass of water, hoping to lessen the chance of my lips swelling like a Botox shot gone wrong. And I used gloves. And I first made a video of my final good-byes, because I was still unsure if it was super brave or the stupidest thing I'd ever done.

I didn't die (clearly). My insides didn't itch. I survived a full twenty-four hours with no reaction and finally let out the breath I had been holding since downing itty-bitty poison in a cup.

I've spent almost a year now working my way up in leaf-piece sizes as Jim suggested. In that time I've been wondering what other information the old-timers possess that would make my life richer, my path smoother, the heartache easier. The lines creasing Jim's face remind me that his generation won't be around forever. Before they graduate to the next life, what tips could they give me—even if they sound kooky—that would help me be more resilient, understand God better, or love others well?

It's good to learn about life from those who have lived it a little longer than us.

I guess that's what inspired this book. I'm not a perfect social feed of good choices, wild success, or polished beauty. But I've lived some life. And I think I've got a tip or two that could help you live the best, brightest version of yours. (Even if the advice sounds straight-up crazy at first!)

Are you the type of person who cares where her life is headed? If so, and if you're brave enough, try putting some of these tips into practice. The results might surprise you. But even if the outcomes aren't perfect, you don't have much to lose by trying. It's not like I'm suggesting you eat a poisonous plant or anything.

Ready? Then let's go.

Love,

Jessie

> DISCLAIMER: I'M NOT A MEDICAL PROFESSIONAL. YOU CAN'T SUE ME IF YOU TRY THIS MADNESS AND END UP WITH POISON OAK DOWN YOUR INTESTINES, OKAY? I WILL DECLINE TO COMMENT . . . AFTER BLAMING JIM.

Tips About Boys

Whether you're convinced guys are dumb, can't stop thinking about them, or wish you knew *what* you thought, there's a reason we're tackling the topic of boys first: because guys tend to hold a lot of sway in a girl's heart. Also, because we can. (And I somehow doubt you're mad at it.)

Tip #1

Appreciate the difference between admiration and attraction.

I signed up because I wanted to serve God. Honestly, I did. But when I got to the tropical island of Antigua for our three-week mission trip, my focus was hijacked faster than you can say *summer crush.*

Our assignment was to run a day camp for local kids. Yarn crafts, cheesy Bible skits, water fights—all the good stuff. In the afternoons and evenings, we worked for the local missionaries, and on the weekends, they took us on adventures like free diving for conch shells in the Caribbean and exploring remote, palm-lined coves.

The problem was, it didn't take long to notice that one of the young missionaries was pretty darn cute. Athletic too. Led worship on his guitar. Obviously loved God enough to follow Him anywhere. Sheesh, he could even dance! Before I knew it, I had myself a new mission: get Mister Missionary to fall for me. I spent most of the three weeks fighting a losing battle against distraction, concocting reasons to work on the same projects, and trying to look my best despite tropic-force humidity.

Granted, crushing fast for someone wasn't exactly out of the ordinary. I was a certifiable *crushaholic* from a very early age. I had a new J +_ = ♥ scribbled on my notebook every few weeks in elementary school. By college, I could no longer count the number of my crushes/relationships on my fingers and toes combined. And, as I've just confessed, I could fall for someone within days—even on a mission trip.

I don't blame you if you're now questioning whether I'm a trustworthy guide. But I'm braving this confession because 1) I know I'm not alone, and 2) I think I finally understand why.

It wasn't that I was flighty, shallow, or addicted to that new-love feeling. The truth is, I got admiration and attraction confused. I assumed they were the same thing. If I had known the differences then, I may have avoided a slew of crushes, and kept my mind on the real mission of that trip.

Admiring simply means noticing a person's positive qualities. You might think, *Wow, his smile could melt ice in a snowstorm.* Or, *He makes me feel seen in a world that ignores me.* Or even, *He's so in love with Jesus!* You think positive thoughts about the person because they're likable or exceptional in some way.

Admiration isn't bad; we're hardwired for it. Part of being made in God's image means we appreciate beauty, strength, empathy, and other qualities that reflect God Himself. And those of us golden retriever types who enjoy people in general find lots to admire!

Attraction, on the other hand, begins with admiration but shifts the focus to possession: *I can only enjoy that good thing if it belongs to me. I want him to smile at me like that.* Or, *I won't be happy unless he sees me as more than a friend.*

Attraction isn't necessarily bad either. If God didn't give us a longing to be more than friends with someone, there would be no couples, marriages, or families. But when we want to "make mine" every guy we admire, when we let our attraction run unchecked, or when we're attracted to trouble, then heartache follows.

Imagine the freedom if you could recognize you admire someone and leave it at that. In other words, to admire without desire. For one, you'd avoid becoming a crushaholic like I was. Two, you would be more discerning in your choice of a boyfriend or husband.

And three, you'd be less likely to cheat on someone you love. Why? Because the part of you that notices admirable qualities in others doesn't turn off once you're married. You'll still meet other guys with gorgeous bods or endearing personalities. If you haven't learned to separate admiration from attraction, you might find your heart pulled away from your truest love.

So go ahead and admire. Compliment God on the nice job He did designing that guy who catches your eye. But take your time getting to know him—his strengths and weaknesses—before deciding whether to scribble your initials inside a heart.

Time to Shine

- Think about that guy you have a crush on (or, if you don't have a crush, someone who at some point had you dreaming). What specific qualities do you admire about him?
- Can you appreciate that guy's positive qualities even if he's never your boyfriend?
- If you shifted your focus from making him "yours" to wishing the best for him, how would that free you up to live your brightest life?

Tip #2

Don't settle for less than you deserve just to get what you want.

John was the star of the college basketball team. Helplessly handsome. Quiet (read: intriguingly mysterious). But it wasn't his effortless blond hair, dreamy smile, or shy eyes that kept my attention. Well, I mean, those weren't the only reasons I was crushin'. His character spoke volumes too. He avoided the party scene, loved God, and respected himself and others. Basically, he was the kind of guy you not only wished you could date, you dreamed of spending your life with him. The kind of guy you hoped would find you worthy to be his.

John could have had his pick of the girls in his unofficial fan club, but he didn't seem interested in any of them. Which honestly just made him all the more crushable. Except, unfortunately, his indifference meant he didn't give me the time of day either.

I was convinced we'd be great together, so his disinterest didn't stop me from driving to away games to watch him play. It didn't ground the butterflies that erupted when I ran into him after class. And it certainly did nothing to stop the hope that, someday, he'd see me as more than a friend.

Months passed. A bunch of my friends got boyfriends. I was insecure and tired of waiting. John still didn't show any special interest in me, and loneliness made me question whether I would ever be beautiful, fun, or godly enough to catch the attention of someone like him.

John had a brother. Alan was opposite of John in pretty much every way. He played a different sport. Average looks. I'm not sure if he had a relationship with God. He was friendly but loud, and had a reputation for being interested in *quite a few* girls. Which was unfortunate . . . except, luckily, that number included me.

In hindsight, I see bright red warning flags waving me down during several of our interactions. But honestly, at the time it felt good to be noticed, singled out, wanted. His attention soothed my loneliness and made me feel like I belonged somewhere, to someone. So I closed my eyes to the rest.

One night as I was walking across campus alone, Alan happened to run into me. We joked, he flirted. Before I realized the danger, he was leading me to a secluded place to "talk." It didn't take long to realize he wasn't interested in conversation. For better or worse, I have a fiery personality, and that night God gave me the presence of mind to get out of that dimly lit dugout before Alan got past a few kisses.

But my temporary lapse in judgment had consequences, even if they could have been more serious. Soon after, I heard that Alan had bragged to his brother (among others) about the rendezvous. If I had ever had any chance with John—the kind of guy I was actually interested in—it was officially roadkill.

In your search for love, sometimes you might feel like your "ideal" guy or relationship is out of reach. In those moments, it can be so hard to wait for God's best gift and His best timing. But take it from me: relationship shortcuts never satisfy the way you hope they will, and they always have consequences. So don't get involved with a guy because he's convenient, you're lonely, he's hot, or your friends think you should. No matter how bad you're tempted, don't settle for less than you deserve just to get what you want in the moment. The kind of guy you dream of spending your life with is worth waiting for—even if it takes a lifetime.

Time to Shine

Some of us have a hard time believing we deserve more than cheap attention, especially if it seems like we've been waiting for Mr. Right for actual ever. Write a letter to your future self, describing the kind of guy that's worth waiting for, and remind her why she's better off waiting for the "right one" rather than settling for "someone." Seal it with love and put it somewhere you'll find it a year or two from now.

Tip #3

Treat your brothers in Christ like brothers, because they are.

A friend of mine always wanted an older brother. You know, someone to teach her how to throw a football, intimidate potential dates, and explain the mysteries of a teenage guy's psyche. As one of five sisters, she felt cheated out of the experience.

I, on the other hand, grew up with three older brothers. You know, someone to throw the football farther than I could run, mock my choice of dates, and thoroughly confuse me with their male teenage psyche.

But, I admit, there were also times when "the boys" (as I called them) proved that God did give me brothers on purpose. One example stands out in my memory.

Ian, the middle of the boys, is four years older than me. When I was in high school, he had already graduated and was making his way in the world. One of my favorite memories, maybe of my life, was the time he drove several hours home specifically to take me on a "date." He wanted to show me how a girl should expect to be treated, and he did. He opened doors and paid for dinner, took me miniature golfing, and asked thoughtful questions about my life. It might have been one date, but that night influenced my outlook and my choices forever.

I'm grateful for the ways all of my brothers have loved me, broadened my thinking, and toughened me up. A good brother can change our lives for the better. A good sister does the same.

Of course, not all biological families have healthy relationships. Sin has messed with God's design, and our sin against each other can leave permanent scars. But here's the good news: if you've made Jesus Lord of your life, you've joined a big faith family. That means you get lots more mothers, fathers, sisters, and brothers to do life with.

If you're lucky enough to have Jesus-loving guy friends in your circle, enjoy the benefits of the extra brothers. Laugh at their jokes, play pickup basketball, and listen to their views about the world. Breathe a sigh of relief when they don't overreact to something careless you said. Appreciate the strengths your "brother friends" bring to the table. Learn from them.

As a sister in Christ, you've got a lot to offer the guys in your world too. Point out the good you notice, teach them how to treat a girl well, remember their birthdays, help them put words to their emotions. Let them know (kindly) when they do something uncalled for.

With all the benefits of family to enjoy, there's really no reason to rush into romance. But since we're talking about guys and girls here, sometimes romance shows up uninvited. If your feelings move beyond friends, here's a super important truth to remember: You're still family. Regardless of what other titles come (like boyfriend/girlfriend), you're still brother and sister in the family of God.

So how can you treat each other like family even when you're exploring a dating relationship? Here are some questions (*not* rules) to get you thinking:

- How would you dress if you were hanging out with your brother?
- What things would you talk about? Avoid talking about?

- How would you act?
- Would you expect him to give you all of his time and attention?
- How would you show affection? (Hugs? Kisses? What kind?)

It might sound weird, old-fashioned, and detrimental to your love life. But this sibling-till-you're-married philosophy will help you establish healthy boundaries as you date, sparing you tons of heartache, deepening your relationships, and screening out potential losers hiding on your "love interest" list. There's not much to lose by trying the family approach. Any guy worthy of your heart will respect you for having boundaries and try to understand your reasons why—just like a brother would.

Time to Shine

- What excites you most about the idea of having a faith family that includes brothers?
- What's one way you could be a good sister to a "brother friend" this week?
- Over the coming week, take mental notes of anything you learn from a guy in your life.

Tip #4

Be a student of the guys around you, so when it's time to date you'll ace the class.

Out of the approximately 2,872 hours I spent in school, my favorite class of all time was Travel Writing 101. Doctor Simons, my college writing professor, created it specially for me so I could attend a semester-long study abroad program in Central America and still graduate on time. As I sat across the desk in his office, Doc (as we affectionately called him) explained that I would be required to read some books over the summer, then document the three and a half months I'd spend exploring four countries.

"Credit for journaling my travels?" My voice did nothing to hide my excitement. If people hugged Doc Simons (which we didn't), I would've squeezed that old, gruff, teddy bear of a man right then and there.

"It better be good," Doc warned over my excited squeals. "I want concrete images." He tapped the desk with the flat of his palm, punctuating each syllable. "No flowery fluff."

I promised him I'd give those *National Geographic* writers a run for their money and tucked a Strathmore one-hundred-page unlined notebook into my Kelty backpack. The world would be my classroom, and I wasn't about to miss a lecture.

In the coming months, the empty pages filled with thousands of words. I took Doc's instructions to heart. Instead of ranting on about my emotional ebbs and flows, I studied absolutely everything around me, from broad strokes to the smallest details. The cracked blocks under vibrantly painted murals downtown. The howl of monkeys hidden in treetops. Fragrant arroz con pollo simmering in modest kitchens. The slimy-sweet fruit inside a "hairy" red rambutan. Ordinary things seen with intentional eyes exploded with wonder.

The people fascinated me too. My Costa Rican "mamá," Jenny, who supported herself and two grown daughters by sewing vests and making alterations. A group of resilient Cuban teens who fingered guitar strings like maestros and knew more American songs than I did. Two compassionate young German women who volunteered at an orphanage in Guatemala City. An older Nicaraguan man who carved clay blocks out of a pit nine hours a day to make thirty cordobas (about $2.25) for his family. As I paid attention to particulars, even the other American students became terribly interesting—like "Tex," a quiet guy who bought nearly every textile peddled in the city of Managua because he felt so bad for the street children who sold them. Or Dave, who somehow forgot where he lived.

Travel Writing 101 permanently changed how I view the world and the people in it. When you get curious, watch closely, and ask good questions, you can learn so much *about* and *from* others.

That skill comes in handy in the world of dating and relationships too. There's a class I suggest you enroll in: "Datability 101." The syllabus? Spend time observing the guys around you.

Pay attention to details. How do they act? Talk? Look for patterns that hint at a guy's character. Is he honest? Respectful? Watch guys who are "taken" too—how do they treat their girlfriends? How do they act when their girlfriends aren't around? Take Doc's advice and keep your emotions out of this class as much as possible. There's a time for falling head over heels, but for now, just focus on being an impartial observer.

The goal of the class? Well, it's not to get a guy by Friday, but Datability 101 will help you learn *about* guys and *from* them over time. As you observe their behavior, you'll see what lies beneath the cute exterior or magnetic charm, so you'll be less likely to fall for a fake. And then, if the right one does come along, you'll recognize him as the gem he is. In other words, be a student today, and when it's time to date, you'll know exactly what you're looking for.

Time to Shine

Start studying! We'll talk more about red flags and other warning signs later in Tip #12. For now, let's focus on the positive qualities you observe in the guys around you. What do you consider nonnegotiable in a potential boyfriend or husband? How do those qualities look in real life? Start a list and add to it as you observe the good, the bad, and the perplexing.

Tip #5

Defining a relationship takes courage, but you deserve to know when you're in one.

I met Cal my first week at college. Amidst the craziness of freshman orientation, he reminded me of my guy friends back home. He was articulate, laughed easily, and was just goofy enough to keep his good looks from going to his head. Cal was also part of a group of us who hit it off that week, and we bonded over beach trips and study sessions. As months passed, we started talking one-on-one. He made sure I had a ride to our group antics, invited me to go Christmas shopping (just the two of us), and made sure to sit by me at church. Others started noticing us pair off, which only confirmed my suspicion that we were nearing couple status. Surely, he'd ask me to be his girlfriend any day.

More months passed, and he still acted more-than-friends, but no official question came. Then one day, he invited me and the crew to his house after church. I was eager to meet his mom, a woman I had heard a lot about. I hoped she'd like me—I mean, what if she was my future mother-in-law? But as she and I talked in her kitchen, two things became super clear: 1) She had no idea that her son and I were, well, whatever we were, and 2) Anyone Cal dated would need to be classier, prettier, and definitely holier than me to pass her twenty-point inspection.

I have a hunch she had a little talk with her son later, because instead of making "us" official, he backed away as slowly and casually as he had entered my life. I can laugh about it now, but at the time, I was hurt and confused. I felt like we were breaking up, but since we were never actually dating, I was left with lots of questions and zero closure.

Can you relate? You like someone, feel there's more than a friendship there, but he never really makes a move. On the other hand, maybe you know deep down that a guy likes you, but you're keepin' it chill because he's fun to hang out with and you don't want to lose a friend or hurt him by telling him no.

Most relationships will have a season between truly "just friends" and something officially more. But if you find yourself in a situationship—straddling the line between casual friendship and committed relationship for seemingly ever—you owe it to yourselves to get clarity.

How? Well, start by asking yourself some tough questions, like:

- Where exactly do I hope this relationship will go?
- Am I sure this person is what I'm really looking for?
- What evidence do I have that he wants to be more than friends?
- Do people I trust agree that he's acting interested?

If you're then sure you'd be down for a relationship, decide how you'll protect your heart, body, and reputation while you're in that space between friends and something more. Ask yourself:

- How much time should I spend texting or hanging out with him?
- How deep will our conversations go?
- Will we spend time one-on-one or in groups?
- How long am I willing to wait to make this official before I move on?

Then it's time to dig deep and be brave. I'd recommend talking to him in person if you can, but maybe first write out what you want to say for practice.

- Explain what you observe. For example: "I'm getting the feeling you like me because . . ."
- Be honest and specific about what you want. For example: "I'd like to stay friends," ". . . get to know each other better," or ". . . see if a relationship might work out."
- Share your boundaries. If he needs more time "in between" to figure it out, that's okay. But it's also okay (and healthy) for you to protect your time, emotions, and reputation. Let him know your limits, kindly but in crystal clear terms.

Tackling a situationship head-on takes courage and honesty, but it usually turns out for the best. After all, you deserve to know when you're in a relationship!

Time to Shine

If you're watching a friend spin their wheels in a situationship, what can you do to help? It's amazing how a fresh set of eyes and impartial opinion can help bring clarity to a confusing situation. We're all more courageous when we have support—and accountability—to do the right thing. That's what friends are for.

Tip #6

A relationship opens your heart to pain, but love is worth the risk.

I wish I had never met him! I cried into my pillow. The soul-deep ache in my heart left me hollow, like someone I loved had died. I didn't want to eat and I couldn't sleep. My eyes had run out of tears days before. *How can it be over?*

For three years, my boyfriend and I had been the high school couple all our friends expected to go the distance. We met at church, and our friendship deepened over time. It seemed we were perfect for each other. When he asked me to be his girlfriend, my stomach did fifteen cartwheels. In the months, then years, that followed, I fell for him even more as we bonded over Friday night football games, school dances, youth group retreats, and lazy summer days. We were each other's first date, first kiss, and first real relationship. That meant we sort of taught each other how to communicate, work out fights, resist jealousy, and treat someone well. In a word, we taught each other how to *love*. When I thought about the future, he was in it. Now that we had broken up, the future just looked empty.

In the fog of those early days, I couldn't imagine moving past the devastation. I wasn't sure I could recover from losing someone who had become so much a part of me. Since it wasn't for forever, was the relationship all a waste of time?

Have you ever flown on an airplane and looked out the window during takeoff? At first, you can make out every detail of every building, even tell the color of the cars on the freeway. But the more minutes that pass—and the farther you fly—the smaller what's behind you seems. You find yourself looking forward, toward the horizon.

Time creates distance from painful situations too, and distance brings a different perspective. Healing came slowly in the weeks that followed, but it did come. In time, I was able to see our three-year relationship from a different perspective. No, it didn't last forever, but it was a class God used to teach me a lot about myself and how He intended relationships to work (1 Corinthians 13–style). Our relationship gave me a friend to share life with. It helped build my confidence, taught me to be less selfish, and opened my eyes to the beauty of God's romantic heart. Despite the painful ending, it *was* worth it.

To avoid all pain, one must avoid all love (and even that comes with its own pain, so there you have it). Sure, you can minimize the hurt by making smart choices in the guy, the pace, and the intensity of your relationship. But if you build a wall of protection around your heart and vow never to let anyone inside, you'll keep out some of God's greatest gifts. God is love, and since we're made in His image, love's in our nature too (see Genesis 1:26 and 1 John 4:7–12). A broken heart might hurt like hades, but time will help put it in perspective. In the end, I think you'll find love is worth the risk.

Time to Shine

- Have you ever had your heart broken by a relationship?
- Looking back, what did you learn? (What did you do well, what do you wish you had done differently, etc.?)
- Would you risk opening your heart again to the right person at the right time? Why or why not?

Tip #7

Mystery is magical. Keep yours as long as possible.

As "The Final Countdown" blared over the venue's speakers, the magician waltzed to center stage. Through smoke and spotlights, she held out her hands and stood still to allow her assistant to lock handcuffs around her wrists and ankles before she stepped into a treasure chest–like box. The assistant then pulled the lid shut over the magician's head and clicked the lock with practiced, dramatic flair. A giant screen counted down from twenty, and the audience shouted along.

Nineteen, eighteen ...

I held my breath. *Could she do it?* This wasn't David Copperfield, after all—this was just my friend Megan, who to this point had kept her ability to do magic a complete secret. At least, for the sake of the five hundred women gathered at the retreat, I *hoped* she actually knew magic. If she didn't pop out of that trunk when the timer ended, the whole audience would feel awkward for her.

Three, two, one ...

The screen hit zero with a digital display of fireworks. The lid opened. And Megan rose to her feet, holding two sets of cuffs.

I jumped to my feet and cheered, as surprised as everyone else. How did she *do* it? Obviously, I knew there was *some* logical explanation, but I couldn't have told you what it was—not even if my life depended on it.

I'm a sucker for a good magic trick. I mean that not just in the sense that I find great delight in being wowed by a well-executed illusion, but also in the less flattering sense that I'm the "sucker" every budding magician hopes is in the audience. I'll watch every move intently, yet completely fail to figure out how he or she did it. Doesn't matter if I'm watching an expert magician at a high-priced, velvet-seat theater show or if I'm at the kitchen table with a six-year-old testing out a card trick. When the woman levitates or the ace appears at the top of the deck, I gasp and clap like a four-year-old watching her uncle pull a quarter from behind his ear. I'm completely mesmerized by magic.

The audience at our women's event loved every moment of the show too. Everyone loves magic. You know why? Because everyone loves a good mystery. We're intrigued by things we can't figure out. Things yet to be known.

Mystery itself is magical.

Keeping a little mystery in our romantic relationships can heighten the magic as well. We're intrigued by things we don't completely understand about the other person. It keeps us wanting more. So as much as we want to know everything about a new love interest, and want them to know everything about us, slowing our roll allows the magic to linger.

That means you don't have to share everything about yourself in the first forty-eight hours after he asks you out. You can take your time responding to his messages when you're busy, wait to share your future hopes or childhood fears, and gradually reveal how deeply you care. Instead of driving him away, showing restraint will likely make him intrigued to know more.

Mystery also keeps physical touch magical. Wondering what your first kiss will be like can supercharge the air when you're in the same space. Once it's normal to feel his lips pressed to yours, some of that magic dissipates. Then you tend to wonder about the next thing you *don't* know. I'm not saying you should or shouldn't ever kiss someone you care about, only that once you do, you can't go back to not knowing. So take your time and enjoy the mystery.

We long to know and be completely known by another human being, and that *is* the eventual goal of a lifelong relationship. Just don't rush to get there. Enjoy the process of discovering the little mysteries about each other. Let the magic linger.

Time to Shine

- If you've been in a relationship before (or are in one now), think about how quickly you passed certain milestones. Did you share a lot of yourself quickly? Too little or too late? What can you learn from that experience for the future?
- If you haven't been in a relationship, based on your personality, do you think you'd be more likely to share too much or too little about yourself with someone you had feelings for?
- What are some practical ways a couple could find a good balance between enjoying the fun of growing close to each other and keeping some mystery alive?

Tip #8

Set physical boundaries before you're in a relationship or your relationship will influence your boundaries.

After spending ten years fighting the Trojan War, the mythical Greek hero Odysseus was understandably exhausted. Anxious to see his family, he gathered his men and set sail for his home island, Ithaca. Unfortunately for everyone on board, the ill-fated journey would make them want to climb back into that old Trojan horse and suck their thumbs. Just about every jealous goddess, vengeful monster, and disgruntled god in the ancient world (and underworld) wanted them dead.

At one point in their journey, a wily minor goddess named Circe fell deeply in love with Odysseus. It was great news for him, because she warned of some coming dangers and explained how to avoid being killed by the sirens. The sirens were birdlike women who appeared beautiful and whose song was so tantalizingly sweet that no man could resist being lured to their island. Once there, the poor chaps would starve to death on account of never wanting to leave. Circe was hoping to see Odysseus again someday, so she gave him a few tips and a big block of beeswax and sent him and the boys on their way.

Odysseus appreciated Circe's advice. The problem was, he *really* wanted to hear the sirens' song. His curiosity burned. *What would it sound like? What promises would they make him?* Still, he accepted that as a mortal man, once he heard the sirens' song, he'd be no match for his own desire. He knew his limitations, so he planned ahead for his protection.

While he still had control of his mind, Odysseus instructed his men to tie him to the ship's mast, so tight he couldn't break free. Under no circumstances were they to untie him, regardless of how he pleaded, raged, pouted, or sweet-talked. Then he busted out Circe's block of beeswax and told the crew to fill their ears so they wouldn't hear the song.

The sirens came. As their sweet song swept across the ship, Odysseus was driven mad with longing. He strained against his bonds until the ropes cut his skin. But his men followed orders. Since they couldn't hear him *or* the song, they rowed and rowed until they came safely through.

Sheer willpower wouldn't have been enough to keep Odysseus from forgetting all his convictions and instead following the sirens. But because he made a plan beforehand that literally kept him from following his passion, he eventually made it home—his heart's truest desire.

When you're in a romantic relationship, physical desire acts a lot like a siren's song. Even though you have convictions, an irresistible blend of love and hormones easily overrides your better sense. You might think you won't cross a certain line, but when your body is pressed against a guy you're head over heels for, you might be surprised by the strong pull to immerse yourself in the melody. In marriage, that's a beautiful part of intimacy. But when you're dating, that powerful force can take you places you swore you'd never go.

You might be strong, smart, and sold out for Jesus, but you're still mortal. Know your limitations, and plan ahead for your protection. While you're clearheaded (ideally before you're even in a relationship, but *definitely* before you lock lips), make a plan that will literally prevent you from being able to act on desire's siren song. As Odysseus learned, even heroes need boundaries to keep them sailing toward their truest desire: in this case, a relationship that glorifies God.

Time to Shine

Consider these practical tips for "tying yourself to the mast." Put a star next to any you want to use in your own life. Add any others you think of.

- Avoid being alone together, especially if you're likely to stay alone.
- Keep the lights on.
- Actually talk about what you're okay with and not okay with. (Holding hands? Kissing? Making out?) It might feel awkward, but clear boundaries are important.
- If you're not sure *what* you're okay with, ask yourself some tough questions like, *Will this go against any clear boundaries God has explained in the Bible? If this relationship ends, will I have regrets? What would I feel comfortable with if I knew my parents would find out?*
- Invite a few trusted people to ask nosy questions about your relationship. Even Odysseus needed others' help to resist.
- Remember that physical desire isn't a *supernatural* siren song. Even if you find yourself in a heated moment, you *do* have the power to step away and insist that he does too.

Tip #9

Confessing you like him rarely ends like the movies. Weigh the risk wisely.

Let's say there's this guy you like. Maybe you've been friends for a long time, and then one day you suddenly realize he means the world to you. Or maybe he's the new kid, full of charm and mystery, that keeps hijacking your thoughts. Every day that passes, you find something else to admire about him. You notice when he walks into a room and get butterflies when he talks to you. You just know you'd be perfect for each other . . . but does he?

He hasn't said anything to you, but—is it your imagination, or did he smile when he caught your eye? He could have asked his friend about the homework assignment, but he specifically found you after class instead. As time passes, your feelings keep expanding to fill the space created by his silence. What if he's interested in you but too shy to say so? Or waiting to spill his feelings until he's one hundred percent sure you like him?

Should you confess that you *do*?

Let's say you decide these torturous feelings are better out than in. Besides, isn't it *dishonest* not to tell him the truth? So you ask if you can talk to him after school—or you write a note or send a text—and bare your vulnerable soul. At that moment, there are really only four ways he could respond . . .

SCENARIO 1: Relieved, he confesses he's a sucker for you. He was just convinced you didn't feel the same way. (Win! Although, if you had dropped some subtle hints, might he have realized you liked him as more than friends and made the first move?)

SCENARIO 2: He was planning to tell you how much he likes you, but was waiting for the perfect moment to tell you. You beat him to it. (Yikes. If you were patient a little longer, you might have had the teen-movie-spectacular moment you were hoping for!)

SCENARIO 3: He's liked you for a while but lacked the courage to say something. (Hmmm . . . Any guy worth your heart should have to put some effort into sweeping you off your feet. If he isn't willing to do that, maybe he's not the one for you.)

SCENARIO 4: He lets you know he doesn't like you in that way. (Bummer. There's a good chance he's going to act a little awkward around you now, not wanting to lead you on or hurt your feelings.)

One in four chances you get a positive-ish outcome. Hmm. The odds aren't necessarily in your favor.

So, should you make the first move? I mean, yeah, you technically can. It's not a sin or anything. But ask God first, and weigh the risks. Sometimes we let our big butterfly feelings convince us there's something there when there isn't. Then, our impatience to have what we want can end up undercutting a relationship instead of sparking one. Guys thrive when they have a quest—a challenge. Allowing him to make the first move lets him show that he can and will lead in a relationship. (Which, if we're honest, most girls would prefer anyway.) If you wait until you have a clear indication that he's into you—namely, he *tells* you—it generally works in your favor.

If you decide to wait, keep studying his character and pray for wisdom, so that if he does eventually confess his feelings for you, you'll know whether he's worthy of yours.

Time to Shine

If you're still wondering whether you should tell your crush that you have feelings for him, ask God for wisdom to help you answer these questions first:

- If I had a choice, would I rather he make the first move?
- What are my motives? Am I impatient to have what I want or tired of waiting around to see if he'll get up the nerve to ask me out?
- What could I gain by waiting? (For example, you could get to know him more, or let him find his courage.)

Tip #10

If you want a guy to act like a guy, actually let him act like a guy.

When Paul and I were newlyweds, we rented a cute, itty-bitty house in a California beach town. One unusually warm Saturday afternoon, the house got a little toasty. In that part of California, hardly anyone has air conditioning, so we opened the windows to try to catch a coastal breeze. When the temperature rose so high that sweat began to trickle down my back, I marched to the front door and swung it open for more air. My man wasn't a fan of this idea, since we didn't have a screen door. Per usual, he was most concerned about the safety of leaving our home unguarded. But I whined and pouted until I persuaded him to leave it open.

All was well (and somewhat cooler) until something large and hairy darted through the front door, past our spots on the couch, and toward the hallway. Now, I'm a strong, usually unflappable woman, but I have *a thing* about rodents, and as soon as I saw that whatever-it-was had a long, smooth tail, I jumped up onto the couch like a cartoon maniac.

"Get it!" I half shrieked, half laughed, the way you do when you're so terrified you start giggling.

My brave knight sprung into action. He chased that rat (aka, Rodent of Unusual Size) all the way to the kitchen. From my perch on the couch, this is what I heard:

"I think it's in the stove. I hear it . . . in the top, by the burners. I'm going to lift the lid and see if I can spot him . . . Ahh!" *Slam.* "Uh, I found him . . . I slammed it on his head. He's stuck, but still moving . . . Where's that big knife?" *Whack!* "Ugghhh, gross! Okay, he's definitely dead now."

Eyes wide from the commentary, I tiptoed to the kitchen and found my shirtless husband and half the kitchen splattered in blood, like he had just reenacted a scene from *Braveheart*. He looked incredibly proud of himself.

Trying to ignore the mutilated rat hanging limp on my stove, I glared at the object in his hand.

"You used my *kitchen knife*?"

Yeah, Paul chased down my worst nightmare, challenged the fiend to a duel, and rose the victor. But I—the coward who spent the ordeal standing on the couch—found fault in which knife he used.

I've had to learn that sometimes bravery makes a mess.

If we want guys to stand up for what's right, act like gentlemen, and lead with courage, we might have to cut them some slack when they don't do it exactly the way we girls want it done. If we want them to become men who will provide for their families, challenge injustice, protect the innocent, and stay involved with their kids, that means we have to let them become actual men. And men sometimes make us scratch our heads. When their guy-ness rubs us the wrong way, we have to ask ourselves whether our irritation is fair, or a personal problem.

Did you know that our greatest weaknesses are often byproducts of our greatest strengths? For example, the same testosterone that gives a man more muscle mass makes him more susceptible to anger. His drive to provide for his family can tempt him to work too much. That passion for justice and righting the world's wrongs can lead to a preoccupation with politics or war. If we strip men of their manhood, we risk losing the good along with the bad.

Hear me: "Boys will be boys" is never a license to hurt or take advantage of others. Never. We also each have the ability and responsibility to work on our weaknesses and grow, with Jesus's help. But if you want your boyfriend, brothers, guy friends, and father figures to stand up and be brave, honest, sacrificial, whole-hearted men, *allow them* to be men. Yes, you are a strong and capable young woman, but you don't have to do everything on your own. Allow them to look out for you, even when you don't think you need protecting. Let them open doors or stare down the bully. Be patient if they talk too much about cars, video games, or football, and be gentle when they don't know the right words to say. Remember, guys have feelings too, so when they're vulnerable enough to talk about the deep stuff, hear them out.

We should absolutely call guys on it when they get true manhood wrong, but let's also thank them when they get it right. Because, even if they do use the wrong knife sometimes, aren't we glad when they're willing to get their hands dirty?

Time to Shine

- How would you describe healthy masculinity?
- Think about the men in your life: family, friends, church leaders, coaches, etc. What examples do you see of those traits?
- Setting aside the way sin has messed us all up, what do you appreciate most about the way God designed men?

Tip #11

We'll all spend time at a table for one. Dress it with flowers.

I met Natalia on the tiny island of Mo'orea, at a small French hostel at the end of a bumpy dirt road. I had just arrived. She was sipping water at a table for one under a pink plumeria tree. When you're a woman traveling alone, you spot other solo female travelers pretty quickly. Before the day was over we had struck up a conversation, and within an hour felt like old friends. Natalia was a Slovakian in her late thirties living in Canada, working a full-time job that she could largely do from anywhere. So she had learned to travel light and cheap, and had already seen much of the world.

When we realized we'd both be on the island of Tahiti on the same day the following week, we hatched a plan involving one car, one map, and one full circle around the entire island in one day. It was an ambitious itinerary guaranteed to make memories. And make memories we did. We strolled through gardens and stood under a towering waterfall. We bought roadside papaya, filled a jar with sand at Teahupo'o (a famous surf spot), and jumped off a tall bridge into a river near Otuofai with a group of local kids. It was a day for the books.

When we returned to Papeete that night, we tracked down a row of food trucks for a late dinner. Over grilled fish and french fries, we got to talking about life, and the subject turned to love and singleness.

"My mother is always asking me when I'm going to get married," Natalia said, rolling her eyes. "I told her, 'It's not like I'm not trying!'" We both laughed.

Then she grew more thoughtful as she added, "I don't think marriage is the answer to happiness, though. I have many friends who are married but they're not as happy as I am."

I wanted to hear more. I asked, "What would you say makes the difference between a single woman who's miserable, and someone like you—who wants a relationship, but is still out here living her life with joy?"

She leaned back in her plastic chair, thoughtful. Finally she said, "It really comes down to your mindset. You can live a great life and be single. You just have to decide that your life isn't better or worse one way or another—it's what you make of it that counts."

Natalia's life wasn't perfect, but she was certainly making it count.

We soon said our goodbyes, but her words have stuck with me ever since. Not just her words, but a picture of a woman not willing to spend her life *hoping* for a relationship to come so she could start living. No, she was already living, charting a course for her life that included meaningful friendships, adventure, purpose, and joy.

The hard truth is that we'll all spend time at a table for one in life. In fact, most people spend quite a bit of time solo. Boyfriends and girlfriends break up. Unfortunately, divorce happens. Husbands and wives eventually die. I know that might sound depressing, but the point is, that reality doesn't have to wreck you. Being alone doesn't sentence you to misery.

You are a whole, complete person. *You.* Not you plus a boyfriend. Not you plus a future spouse. Yes, a special someone can add a different dimension of joy, but it will also add new dimensions of pain and hard-won growth. Like Natalia said, your life isn't better or worse based on your relationship status—your life is what you make of it.

If God's best for you includes marriage, then make it a good life. If God's best for you includes long stretches of singleness, make it a good life. When you spend time at a table for one, just add a vase of your favorite flowers right there in the middle. Trust God to write your story, then go make some memories.

Time to Shine

It's fairly easy to rattle off a list of benefits that come from being in a relationship with someone. But have you ever stopped to think about the benefits of being single? Take some time to write down five of the emotional, physical, or spiritual benefits that could be yours while you don't have a boyfriend, husband, or kids to consider.

1. _____

_____

2. _____

_____

3. _____

_____

4. _____

_____

5. _____

_____

Tip #12

Warning signs only help if you actually listen to them.

When I started dating Ronnie, it seemed all my prayers for a "perfect match" had been answered. He was cute, kind, talented, and had genuine faith in God. His dad was a pastor, his mom really liked me, and within a month we were already talking about forever. (If you've read "Mystery Is Magical," you know why I wouldn't recommend that last bit.)

In hindsight, maybe the first red flag to appear was how fast he jumped in with both feet, without really knowing me that well. I chalked it up to my amazingness (who wouldn't fall quickly for me?) and his openness to love at first sight (just like the movies!). The next warning sign was how quickly he amped up the physical part of our relationship. I was pretty clear about my boundaries, but it seemed whenever we were together, he would push the limits. Over time, that "pushing" got more aggressive, but I knew he loved me and wanted to marry me. I rationalized, *Boys are just more physical, right?*

Then one night, he told me he had something he needed to share. He said I was the only one he trusted with this information—a secret he had been carrying for years. Through tears, he confessed something he had done to someone else—something criminal. Something the authorities *still* didn't know about, and he had no plans to tell them. That red flag should have sent me running in the other direction. But I was so focused on "us" that I only thought about how I could show him compassion and grace. I rationalized, *He's not that person anymore. He's forgiven.*

In the coming months, more bad habits and sin issues surfaced, but instead of heeding the warning signs, I sped right past them. I knew he loved God and loved me, so I downplayed and rationalized stuff he did. *I can deal with that*, I thought, *because of all his other great qualities.*

He told me he had asked his parents' blessing on a future with me, and that his mom had offered a family heirloom wedding ring. All signs pointed to him popping the question any day.

By the sheer grace of God, instead of proposing, Ronnie suddenly broke things off completely. He said he didn't feel peace about us anymore, like God was telling him to stay away from me.

Thank you, Jesus.

I had ignored every single red flag like a headstrong child. If God hadn't intervened, I would have made a monumental mistake. I know God specializes in redeeming our messes—that nothing we've done or will do falls outside His mercy—but there are still consequences to our choices. I very easily could have said "I do" and spent my life dealing with manipulation, addiction, and a double life.

You're never going to find someone without any faults. You aren't perfection incarnate either! The goal isn't to nitpick every flaw. At the same time, dating (or courtship, or whatever approach you choose) is a time to really evaluate who this person is. Think about it: You're both likely showing your *best* sides during that part of the relationship. If you still see concerns, you'd be smart to pay attention. Because warning signs are only helpful if you're brave enough to face them.

Time to Shine

Sometimes we have trouble knowing the difference between red, yellow, or even beige flags. These examples aren't canon—just a place to start. You can cross out any you don't agree with, and I've left blanks for you to add others.

BEIGE FLAGS	YELLOW FLAGS	RED FLAGS
Personal preference. Not necessarily bad yet worth considering.	Take note, proceed with caution.	Stop, turn around, run the other way!
• Opposite views on minor issues • Age difference (within reason) • Has different hobbies • Different friend group • Long-distance • Not your "type" • • • • • •	• Not much to talk about • Lack of other friend-ships • Addicted to gaming • Avoids working out conflicts • Trouble committing • Insecure • Disrespectful to his parents or friends • • • • •	• Explosive anger, short fuse • Lack of morals (lying, stealing, etc.) • Sexual pressure • Porn use • Substance abuse • Not interested in God • Super religious but no genuine relationship with Jesus • • • • •

Tips About Friends and Family

Sometimes our family and friends can bring headaches and drama, other times they multiply the light in our world. The difference often lies in how we approach the relationships. Whether they come easy or drive you crazy, here are some tips to navigate them well.

Tip #13

Know who you are, or someone else will tell you.

If my "eras" were famous enough to inspire a world tour like Taylor Swift's, there'd be just as many costume changes (though decidedly fewer sequins). I'd regale you with songs from the High School Sweetheart era, inspired by a steady boyfriend, youth group lock-ins, and varsity football games. The Outdoor Enthusiast era, when a group of friends convinced me to buy rock climbing shoes and spend my weekends camping in the desert with coyotes. During the Intellectual era, I'd join the studious elite, wearing a black pea coat and scribbling sappy poetry on the backs of classical concert programs. And to finish off the set, I'd blush through the entire Band Groupie era, in which I followed a cute drummer to all his gigs and found out what really goes on backstage.

I wish I could chalk up these distinct seasons of my life to a girl figuring out her interests. But, perhaps like Taylor's, most of my eras were influenced most by the people in my life—their attention, expectations, approval, and quirks. Basically, my personas changed because of Chameleon's law.

> *Chameleon's law:* A girl not grounded in her own identity will adapt to become like the people around her.

You won't find it in the dictionary (since I might have made it up), but this law strikes as predictably as gravity. Trust me, I'm somewhat of an expert. If you could get a degree in adapting to others, I'd have a PhD.

If you're not familiar with the chameleon, it's a peculiar little reptile with a crazy-long tongue and a remarkable superpower: the ability to shift the hue and brightness of its skin to blend in with its surroundings. If a chameleon lounges on a leaf, for example, within seconds it will sport a vivid green. Climbing up a trunk? Bark-brown it goes. This skill comes in handy when trying to avoid becoming a kestrel's lunch. But in the human world, changing our colors to blend in doesn't always work in our favor.

Our friends, family members, and especially our love interests can hold a lot of sway in our lives. If we're not sure who we are—or who we want to be—their influence will often decide for us. We'll usually take the path of least resistance for the chance to belong. (Bonus tip: since this is partly unavoidable, hang out with people you'd *want* to become more like!)

To have the best relationships with friends and family possible, we'll need to show up as our authentic selves—not the version we think others want or that blends in easier.

You don't have to completely identify all your interests by this weekend. Try new vibes, figure out what "you" feels most authentic, as long as it's in line with your beliefs. Sure, sometimes you'll discover new interests or hobbies based on others' influence. That's great! But you'll have fewer regrets if you intentionally figure yourself out instead of letting others label or pressure you into what they want. After all, God delights in *you,* not who you can pretend to be.

When you look back on your own eras, I hope they were most inspired by your curiosity, convictions, and personal flair. Leave blending in to the chameleons.

Time to Shine

If you're going to *be* who you are, you have to *know* who you are. I wrote the "Me Quiz" to help you start thinking about your interests, character, talents, weaknesses, and dreams. You can download a copy at LifeLoveandGod.com/me-quiz. In the meantime, here are a handful of questions to get started:

1. If I had a Saturday all to myself, I'd spend it _____
   _____.

2. When I think about the future, I feel _____
   _____.

3. I'm proud that I can _____.

4. The people I'm closest to are _____
   because they _____.

5. I'd describe my style as _____
   _____.

6. Someday, I hope to _____.

7. I'd describe my relationship with God as _____
   _____.

8. If I could spend the day with anyone in the world, I'd pick
   _____.

9. I'd describe my personality as _____.

10. My favorite place is _____
    because it's _____.

Tip #14

Be generous. A gift can open the door to friendship.

Christmas of my sophomore year was fast approaching, and I needed just the right gift for a special friend. Something that would say I cared, without being too "extra," you know? Also, it needed to be cheap, because I was flat broke.

One day, I had a lightbulb moment. My art teacher had just started a unit on weaving. What if I wove a little something for my friend? All that remained was deciding what to make. A potholder? Nah, I needed something a high schooler could use. A scarf? Too basic. What about . . . a *blanket*? Yes! Nothing says friendship like a cozy throw.

I grabbed the biggest piece of cardboard I could find, which was approximately the size of a refrigerator, and cut notches along the top and bottom for the warp threads. Two colors didn't seem special enough, so I sketched a four-color pattern, featuring my friend's initials centered in the middle. I purchased a half dozen skeins of yarn and got to work.

And work I did. In my quest for the perfect gift, I severely underestimated how long it would take to weave an entire *blanket* with a single strand-width of yarn. Every time I'd press the finished rows upward to eliminate the holes, I eliminated most of my progress. It was like stuffing a car with cotton balls. That stupid blanket with the crooked initials took six weeks of toil—including eight days of Christmas break—and cost more in yarn than I care to admit.

In a sheer act of stubborn will, I finished it. And let me tell you, it was *extra* in every way. Extra big, extra weird, extra regrettable. In fact, that blanket probably ranks as the worst gift I've ever given. (At least, let's hope so.)

Luckily, gifts don't have to be spectacular to let the other person know you care. And when someone knows you care, it makes them think fondly of you. And when they think fondly of you, they're more likely to want a friendship or relationship. It's a win-win: they get a gift, you score social points. Of course, giving gifts for selfish reasons would be lame, but genuine generosity usually comes with unexpected rewards.

Proverbs 18:16 (NLT) says, "Giving a gift can open doors; it gives access to important people!" The original Hebrew translates the beginning as "a gift makes room." Do you wish a particular friend or group had "room" for you? Do you long for a seat at the table? Bring a gift, without strings, and see what happens.

The gift doesn't need to be over the top either. Years ago, an acquaintance gave me a bouquet of peony flowers after an important interview, and to this day I think of her and smile whenever I see pink peonies. My first birthday in a new town, someone else gave me a set of her favorite gel pens because she heard "the new girl" was a writer. Still, every time I use one, I think of her. Others have opened doors to my friendship with kind words, time, a warm smile, or really good dark chocolate.

Starting (and keeping) relationships can be challenging. A thoughtful gift, given without strings, will not only bring you the joy of giving, but might just open doors for you too.

Time to Shine

- What gifts—given or received—stand out in your memory? What made them special or thoughtful?
- Make a "gift list" of simple items or acts of service that would make someone else feel seen or appreciated. (Some ideas to get you started: a thoughtful note, homework help, a compliment, homemade cookies, a favorite snack, a gift card.)

1. _____

2. _____

3. _____

4. _____

5. _____

6. _____

7. _____

8. _____

9. _____

10. _____

Tip #15

Comparison kills friendships. Pick an attitude of abundance instead.

One summer, I lived in the beautiful state of Washington. Having been born and raised in Southern California (think: permanent drought), the lush green of the Pacific Northwest felt like the Emerald City of Oz. I couldn't get enough of the longer days, sparkling creeks, and towering, snow-capped peaks. That summer, I also discovered another secret about the Northwest.

In Washington, blackberry bushes run amuck like weeds—springing up along roadways, creeping into yards, and poking out of ditches. Now, where I grew up, all tasty fruit was protected by fences, guard dogs, threat of lawsuit, etc. You grow it, you keep it. Imagine my euphoria when this unabashed fruit lover found herself surrounded by acres of a "nuisance" plant that produced real fruit. Tasty fruit. *Free* fruit! Thousands of ripe, juicy blackberries, just begging me to harvest them. I had died and gone to frugivore heaven.

The family I was staying with thought it was cute the first time I went out with a big, steel colander to collect said berries. *Aw, look at that cute Californian,* they mused, *digging around in the thorny weeds.* They smiled politely, even helped me bake a blackberry cobbler for dessert that first night. But when I began returning day after day with bushels of berries, filling their fridge and covering the countertops, they kindly requested I limit my harvests to what I could personally consume in one lifetime.

I *reluctantly* agreed.

When I ventured into the fruitful abundance of the Pacific Northwest with my Californian fruit-scarcity mentality, I felt panicked to get more, more, more, because I worried the bushes would run out of blackberries before I could get my share. I shoveled them into my mouth and filled my buckets for later. I shredded my skin on the thorny canes, reaching deep into the tangle for the biggest, juiciest berries. It wasn't until my hosts assured me that I would always find enough berries that I finally slowed down and enjoyed those I had already picked.

When you know there will always be enough, you tend to slow down and enjoy what you have. You might call it an attitude of abundance. It's acknowledging that God has already given you everything you need to live life for Him (2 Peter 1:3), so you can stop searching for the elusive "more."

Apply that to your friendships, and you'll ward off comparison and jealousy, two nasty friendship killers. How? Well, when I believe I have enough intelligence, beauty, wit, strength, and faith, I can enjoy what I have instead of comparing myself to others. If I have enough, who cares if my skin isn't as smooth as hers? Who cares if he's in the relationship I wish I had? Why worry if she starts hanging out with someone else more than me? I don't have to have *everything*. Just enough.

Now check this out: When I realize I already have *more* than enough, I can be crazy generous with my abundance. Blackberries for everyone! For example, when I recognize the abundant good in me and my situation, I can give my friends compliments, share my stuff, offer my time, and spread happiness like there will always be enough of it. Because there will. An attitude of abundance keeps comparison from taking root, then it inspires us to give freely, helping our friendships flourish—like a bumper crop of summer fruit.

Time to Shine

- In what areas do you find yourself focusing on comparison and feeling jealousy?
- How could an attitude of abundance stop comparison from taking your brightest life from you?
- In light of all that God has already given you, how can you bless others with your abundance this week?

Tip #16

Guy friends can be easier, but you need girlfriends too.

"Nah, Jess is cool. She can stay."

My seventeen-year-old self sat a little straighter against the bus's pleather bench seat and threw a sweatshirt over my sweaty uniform. A few more guys slid in around me. It would be a long ride home from the basketball tournament, but hanging with the guys' team in the back of the bus—instead of with my team in the front—would make the trip entertaining at least.

"How many rebounds?" Jensen asked me.

I grinned. "More than you."

"Ooooh, burn!" Beck laughed.

"Kidding," I said, punching Jensen's arm. "I mean, I did outscore you, but you left it all on the court." He laughed, punching me back.

As the bus lumbered home, we talked about the bad call in the second quarter, the merits of a full-court press, and why Doritos trumped Fritos in our real-time taste tests. I was just one of the guys, and I liked it that way. I could hang with the boys because I played hard, didn't get emotional, and laughed at their dumb jokes. I was a pro at that. After all, I had three older brothers to teach me what guys found funny.

Girl friendships were heavy on drama. "Guys are just easier," I'd tell myself. And that was true. Sort of. *It's complicated.*

When I was young—from preschool till junior high—I hung out with mostly girls at school, church, around the neighborhood. We swung on the monkey bars, made honeysuckle necklaces, and baked lemon bars together. We had our share of petty fights and misunderstandings, but what was the alternative? The boys had cooties and smelled bad.

In high school, something changed. Due (at least in part) to the guys wearing deodorant, they held a new, mesmerizing appeal. At the same time, my girl friendships got tainted by jealousies, judgment, and all-around bad juju. So, except for the girls on my sports teams, I opted to hang with guy friends and/or a boyfriend over my female compatriots. I was drawn to the path of least resistance. But now I see that I was also drawn to something else.

See, as girls, we want to be wanted, we want to feel beautiful, we want to know that we're worth a guy's pursuit. Those desires usually start surfacing around the time we change from little girls into young women . . . yeah, right about the time I inched away from my girlfriends and toward the guy variety. If I'm completely honest, I suspect I was drawn to the boys not just because they were "easier" but also because they complimented me, paid attention to me, and made me feel like I belonged.

Does that mean it's wrong to have primarily guy friends? Not necessarily. We can learn a lot from boys—like the value in taking risks, finding the funny in life, and throwing a proper spiral.

But we also need girlfriends, even if they are one hundred percent more difficult. Just like guys teach us certain things best, girls have a knack for teaching us to be caring, thoughtful, and responsible. They're more likely to listen when we have a hard day, and to call us out when we're being too flirty. How many guys your age can help you wade through the unique perks and challenges of being female, offer solid relationship advice, or help you style your hair for prom? Plus, sometimes you'll need to talk about, well, girl stuff.

And it's good to have at least a couple of friends who don't fall into that "might be a love interest someday" category, you know? Because nine times out of ten, when a guy and girl spend a lot of time together, Cupid eventually muddles things. Tell me I'm wrong.

The Bible doesn't mention the gender of our friends nearly as often as the friendships themselves. So I encourage you to focus on 1) choosing good friends (who point you to Christ, make smart choices easier, and value you, not what you can do for them), and 2) being a good friend. At the end of the day, whether your friends are mostly guys, girls, or a mix, God cares most about the quality of your friendships over their chromosomes.

Time to Shine

- Write down the names of the friends you interact with most (in person or online). What have your guy friendships taught you? How about your girl friendships?
- If you're super honest with yourself, do you see any ulterior motives in your desire to be friends with guys? Girls?

Tip #17

Shared experiences tie the bonds of friendship tighter.

I lugged my giant suitcase through the international airport, weaving through travelers toward the Tower Air ticket counter where we were instructed to meet. A professor who could have passed for Indiana Jones held a sign over his fedora: "Israel Bible Extension Program." About two dozen college students already waited nearby. I noticed a few familiar faces, but only knew one by name. The program would take us 7,586 miles from home to study in the land of the Bible. We were leaving as strangers. I had no way of knowing then, but in three and a half months, we'd return closer than family.

Life on a moshav—a compound where you eat, sleep, study, work, and sauna in community—has a way of familiarizing people. You get to know everyone's names, what they look like when they wake up, and who is already checking out who. Proximity and small talk made us acquaintances, but we bonded—*really* bonded—by doing stuff together.

We learned to trust each other while climbing crumbling towers and navigating Jerusalem with nothing but a backpack and a paper map. We confessed our childhood fears while floating in the Dead Sea and reenacted Jack and Rose's iconic *Titanic* pose while sailing across Lake Galilee. We sharpened each other's faith while praying at the Western Wall and celebrated Easter at the place of Jesus's resurrection. We formed inside jokes while being taught traditional dances and unearthing artifacts from ancient dirt at a real archeological dig. The more we *did* together, the closer we became.

They were the types of friendships I had always wanted—full of laughter, acceptance, and a fair smidge of mischief. The funny thing is, those same students went to college with me back in the States. We had passed each other in the hallways, eaten meals in the same dining hall, and taken many of the same classes together. Yet it wasn't until we started playing, exploring, and venturing outside our comfort zones that we became best of friends.

There's something about shared experiences that can bond total strangers. That's true of big adventures like study-abroad programs, but the same principle applies to everyday life too. Something as simple as taking a hike, biking through town to get ice cream, or picnicking on a Sunday afternoon can tighten the bonds of friendship like few things can. With a little more planning, you could up the friendship ante by attending summer camp, tackling a community service project, or serving on a mission trip together.

Casual conversations and group texts have their place. Laughing with your friends over a funny meme or talking about homework can also be part of a growing friendship. But if you want to take your relationships to the next level, do stuff together. Curate experiences that stretch you, force you to live in the moment, and set the stage for lifelong memories.

Time to Shine

Start an ongoing activity list where you can write down ideas as they come (so you'll never wonder, *What should we do?*). Here are a few to get you started:

- Go geocaching.
- Take a walk, hike, or bike ride.
- Visit a library.
- Make friendship bracelets.
- Go rock climbing.
- Swim.
- Attend a sports game.
- Host a game night.
- Go camping.
- Bake something.
- Draw or paint outside.
- Play a new sport.
- Sing karaoke.
- Choreograph a dance.
- Pick up trash at a park.
- Go stargazing.
- Volunteer at a local nonprofit.

Now, plan one thing to do with at least one person this week.

Tip #18

Loneliness is better than getting caught in a rip current of friend drama.

Blake Spataro was on vacation with his family the summer of his nineteenth year. St. Simon's Island, Georgia, is known for its salt marshes, golf courses, and golden stretches of sand. It's also known to have a wicked rip current at high tide, but that wasn't a thought in Blake's mind as he lounged in the water that evening, enjoying some alone time in the fading light.

Before he realized what was happening, a strong rip current began pulling him away from shore. If you don't know the signs to look for, rips are easy to miss and hard to avoid. And this one had Blake's number.

Pulled by a force he felt powerless to resist, he was sucked farther and farther into the ocean. He tried calling for help, but no one heard him. All he could do was try to stay afloat. He treaded water as the sun set and the stars came out. Midnight came and went. When he got tired, he floated on his back and closed his eyes. As the hours passed, his hope sank deeper. He prayed for peace to face the end he felt sure was coming.

Thankfully for Blake, "the end" turned out to be less final than he feared. By early morning, a new current had nudged him toward land. That distant slice of solid ground sent him swimming for shore. Ten *hours* after being tugged out to sea, his feet found sand again.

"Worst vacation ever. But also my most exciting," he told reporters later.[1] I guess you could say that!

What Blake didn't know about rip currents cost him a night in the ocean. See, you don't actually *have to* let the current take you wherever it wants. Even though a rip feels like you have no option but to let the undertow carry you, you *can* get out. Most people panic and try to swim back the way they came—right into the very force pushing them seaward. But if you swim at an angle perpendicular to the current instead (parallel to the beach), you can break free from its hold, then swim toward solid ground.

I've found that friend drama often works like a rip current. If you don't know the signs to look for, it's easy to miss and hard to avoid. Because girls are often more relational, we can easily get caught up in the story of everyone's lives, failings, crushes, betrayals, or whatever. Keeping up with the latest news and who disses who can feel irresistible, like an outside force sucking you into it. And once you're caught in the tow, it's exhausting! But just like with a rip current, you can choose to exit a group of friends who feed on drama. Or better yet, learn to spot the warning signs—like gossip, backstabbing, or cutting humor—and avoid it altogether!

Blake's date with the rip current might have made for an "exciting" vacation, but given the chance, I'd wager he would have chosen a boring night vacationing with his folks over the thrill of nearly drowning. Swimming away from drama usually involves some loneliness, at least for a time, while you look for new friends. But while feeling left out can be painful, you'll likely find it hurts less than the lung-seizing pain of drowning in rumors, cliques, and

---

1. Dominick Proto and Douglas Lantz. "Teen spends 10 hours treading water after a rip current swept him out to sea." ABC News, July 12, 2018. https://abcnews.go.com/US/teen-spends-10-hours-treading-water-rip-current/story?id=56538544, accessed October 10, 2023.

relational betrayal. And the new friendships you find afterward can feel like a strip of land after a very long night.

Time to Shine

- How would you describe "friend drama"?
- Have you personally experienced it?
- If you had to choose, would you pick feeling left out or a sense of belonging despite the drama? Why?

Tip #19

To feel full of love, first learn to fill the cracks.

Once upon a time, a girl named Mari lived with her mother in the desert of Kaja. Each morning of the dry season, Mari would walk three miles with the villagers to a small oasis spring, which bubbled out of the dry earth under a grove of doum palms. There she would fill her clay pot with water, cover the opening—so as not to spill—then make the long, hot journey home. And so, each day, she quenched her and Mother's thirst.

One especially dry season, Mari's mother became ill. Mari didn't dare leave her for hours to walk to and from the spring, yet without water, they would soon both die. Left with no other option, she took the clay pot and ran toward the village. In her haste, she tripped over a stone and dropped the pot against the hard earth. Grateful it hadn't shattered, she dusted it off, then ran until she came to her cousin's house.

"Can you spare a cup of water for my mother?" she asked.

"Yes, of course." Her cousin's family poured a small cup of precious liquid into Mari's clay jar. She covered the opening—so as not to spill—and ran to a friend's house.

"Can you spare some water for my sick mother?" she begged.

"I can do this for you," he replied, and poured a small offering into the jar.

On and on she ran, hut to hut, and each villager responded generously to her need. Soon the jar was full, and covering it—so as not to spill—she rushed home to be with Mother.

Setting the heavy pot on the earthen floor, she poured a cup of water for her mother, took one for herself, and sighed with relief. Then they slept.

The next morning, grateful she would not have to leave her mother to walk to the spring, she returned to the jar. But when she uncovered it, she found it empty. Confused and panicked, she dropped to the ground beside it, and found that her knees sank into *damp* earth.

Lifting the empty jar to the sun, she peered closely through the opening. A thin ribbon of light leaked through the clay, nearly splitting her heart in two. Every gift from her family and friends had seeped through the crack overnight, leaving the jar as dry as the desert of Kaja. Now Mari would have to return to the village, to face each person she had visited the day before and ask them to fill her jar once again.

But first, she would mend the leak. Because a cracked jar cannot hold what it is given.

Sometimes a person can feel unloved because their family and friends genuinely don't show love very well. But in my experience, I've more often felt like an outsider when I've unknowingly had a crack in my jar. In those seasons, others' affection, kind words, likes, invitations, time, and attention didn't fill me up because my heart wasn't capable of holding those good things. They leaked right out.

Okay, that's a nice story, Jessie, but how do you actually repair the cracks? Well, naturally, the first step is to figure out what's causing the leak! In my own life, I've found five common cracks that waste what my friends and family pour into me, making me feel drained and alone.

- **PRIDE:** No matter how much attention and affirmation I get, I deserve more.
- **INSECURITY:** I don't understand my worth, so I need someone else to validate me.
- **BLINDNESS:** I don't see how others are showing me love because I'm not looking for it.
- **SELF-HATE:** I don't deserve their love, so I push it away or minimize it.
- **FEAR:** I've been hurt in the past, and if I let them love me, it could happen again.

Can you relate? Once you've figured out what's causing the leak, it's time to start patching things up. I've found that usually looks like replacing lies with truth. Simple, but not easy! For example:

- *I don't have to be told I'm the best to know I'm a good player.*
- *I'm priceless in God's eyes, which is all the value I need.*
- *My dad invited me fishing to spend time with me—not my first choice, but his way of showing he cares.*
- *I'm worthy of love.*

Life has a way of knocking our hearts around sometimes. Chances are they'll get cracked every now and then. But if you can recognize the leaks and let God help you patch them up, you'll be able to live loved. And a girl who lives loved not only feels full, she also has life-giving love to share with her family and friends.

Time to Shine

What you look for, you'll find. This week, watch for the ways your family and friends show you love. Did someone do something for you they didn't have to? Say something kind? Tease you because they wanted to feel connected to your life? Give you a fist bump or hug? Keep track of them in a note app or journal, as well as your gut reaction. Did you feel loved? If not, do any of those five common cracks I shared need patching?

Tip #20

Live by a Family Manifesto, and you'll leave without regrets.

When I was a kid, my mom was my person. My world. I couldn't even spend the night at someone's house without calling her two hours in to pick me up and take me back home with her.

Then came high school, during which I became largely preoccupied with one, all-encompassing subject: me. I was focused on my grades, my boyfriend, my teams, my agenda. Oh, I still loved my mom, don't get me wrong. But at that time in my life, I was kind of more in love with what she did *for* me. She drove me a million places, made sure I had clothes, took care of me when I was sick, and always listened when I vented about homework, friend drama, or hopes for the future.

The future. It's a funny thing. Sometimes you get so focused on it that you become oblivious to what it may bring.

When cancer took my mom's life, my biggest regret wasn't our fights, though we had some pretty epic door slams. No, my biggest regret was that I shared a roof with the best mom in the world for eighteen years, yet took so many of them for granted. I regret my apathy. If I had known then I'd only get twenty-seven years with her, I would have made the most of each one.

You (probably) won't live at home forever. That might be good news, if the dynamics drive you crazy. Or, if you get along great with your family, the thought of change might terrify you. Either way, like it or not, change will come—maybe slowly, maybe all at once.

Things won't always be as they are now. We'd be wise to live in light of that (see Ecclesiastes 7:2).

If you want to look back on the years you spent at home without regrets, live them intentionally. I pray this Family Manifesto will give you practical inspiration to love the people you call family well.

Family Manifesto

I'll savor each day I have with my family, not knowing how many days I will get.

I'll record happy memories with my camera or journal so I can remember the good times.

I'll forgive quickly because life is too short to hold grudges. I'll use my words to build up instead of tear down.

I'll be thankful for the sacrifices others make for me and tell them so.

I'll practice letting others choose/go first/have the final say instead of insisting on my own way.

I'll pray for my family members because—just like me—God has a plan for each of them.

I'll ask questions about their lives now because I may not always be able to.

I'll take time to just "be" together, without distractions.

I'll look for the good in my family members and tell them when I see it.

I'll try to stay calm even when I'm really upset.

When talking to friends, I'll be quick to point out my
family's strong points instead of their weaknesses.

I'll set a good example for my siblings.

I'll tell my family I love them every chance I get.

I'll thank God for my family every day, even the hard days.

*Taken from *Family: How to Love Them (and Help Them Like You Back)*
by Jessie Minassian. Copyright © 2017.

Time to Shine

Download a copy of the Family Manifesto at https://lifeloveand-god.com/family-manifesto and put it somewhere you'll see it often. Pick one declaration to work on each day for the next two weeks.

Tip #21

All families disagree. Those that love well must learn to fight fair.

I'm a firm believer that, every so often, we should do something that moderately terrifies us. It keeps a person on their toes. This is why, last weekend, I signed up to play paintball. I had never played before for one simple reason: as a general rule, I try to *avoid* high-velocity solid objects being shot toward me. It's a guiding principle that hitherto had served me quite well, because, well, I don't like pain. But since my friends assured me it wouldn't hurt "that bad," I decided it was time to live a better story.

After signing a waiver that had me questioning the wisdom of my decision (as in, "Who should we call in the event of your death?"), I pulled on a mask, filled the gun's hopper with bright-orange pods, and put on my game face. Smacked my chest for good measure. If I was gonna do this, I would do it *Black Hawk Down*–style.

When we got to the course, my courage lasted until approximately the moment I learned the other players consisted of five off-duty first responders. The odds suddenly looked poor, but it was too late to back out. When the referee said *go,* I let pure, unadulterated adrenaline propel me away from the safety of our home fort. I dashed for a stack of giant tires, then ducked under a PVC pipe blind before hiding behind an old washer and dryer, not necessarily trying to shoot the other team as much as avoiding *getting shot.*

I accomplished my goal quite brilliantly for the first few minutes. Eventually, I heard someone from the other team getting closer. I broke cover and took my chances. Somehow, I managed to pelt the guy in the armpit—beginner's luck—but I had given away my position. I felt the sting before I saw the bright-orange spot splat across my shin. I'm not gonna lie, it stung like a drunk hornet. But even though I knew I'd have a decent bruise the next day, I'm here to report I didn't die on the field. Not then, nor after any of the other shots to my person: three to the hand, one to the stomach, and one in that tender spot on the back of my arm. And you know what? I actually had a great time. In fact, by the last round—a game of capture the flag—I was the crazy fool who ran bullheaded into the center of the field to steal the yellow rag from Captain America's shield, winning the game for our team!

Despite my fear going in, the paintball battles served a purpose: I found courage, learned I was stronger than I thought, and walked away better for it.

In family life, battles can serve a purpose too. When you disagree with your parents or siblings, you can find your voice, learn to listen, and walk away better for it. But for family fights to do more good than harm, you have to learn how to fight fair. You could think of it as using paintballs instead of real ammunition. The goal is to avoid seriously wounding someone. For example, you should avoid:

- criticizing things the other person can't change (like making fun of their inability to read well).
- using explicit language.
- saying *always* and *never* (like "You never listen," or "You always screw things up.").
- threatening or causing physical harm.

Instead, "Watch the way you talk. . . . Say only what helps" because "each word [is] a gift" (Ephesians 4:29, *The Message*). What does that look like in practice? To make the battle productive:

- work toward understanding their point of view.
- before speaking, ask yourself, "Is this honest *and* helpful to the conversation?"
- call a cease-fire (take a break) if you're not getting anywhere.
- ask for and offer forgiveness.

Conflict comes with the family territory, and sometimes it brings frustration, hurt, and misunderstanding. The blows might even hurt like a paintball to the buttocks sometimes. But when you avoid deep, permanent wounds, conflict can help a family grow stronger. As you learn to fight fair, you'll be fighting *for* your relationships—which is part of loving them well.

Time to Shine

- When the people you call family disagree, what usually happens? Do you fight fair? Avoid conflict? Go all-out war on each other?
- Which of the keys to healthy conflict mentioned above can you work on this week?
- What suggestions for fighting fair would you add?

Tip #22

Your parents are people too. Get to know them.

MaryAnn was a good girl with a wild side. After growing up in a small Wisconsin town with eight brothers and sisters, she entered her twenties and decided it was time for a change. So she and a girlfriend loaded their cars and made for the West Coast. They had no job prospects, no place to live—just a suitcase full of optimism and the need for a fresh start.

After finally reaching Seattle, they drove south, looking for a city big enough to fit their dreams. When San Francisco filled the horizon, they decided they had found it. They got jobs, found an apartment to rent, and settled in. MaryAnn was determined to make her family proud—to prove she had what it took to succeed. But before too long, her wild side and longing for love landed her in situations similar to the those she had tried to leave in the Midwest. In a twist that threatened to crush her budding optimism, she found out she was pregnant.

This small-town girl, who had mustered all her courage to leave home and make her way in the world, now faced a life-or-death decision: *Should I keep the baby?*

The father didn't think so. He was working through his own issues. Her doctor didn't either—he claimed an abortion would have "the least psychological effects." But MaryAnn was convinced she didn't have the right to take away a life to cover up her mistake. Her parents suggested she give the baby up for adoption, but she wasn't sure she could live with herself, knowing somewhere on earth her child might wonder, "Why didn't my mom want me?" In a crazy act of courage and sacrifice, having no idea how she was going to support another life, she chose to keep her baby.

She named the child Jessica, meaning "Gift from God."

A few months later, she sat in a nearly empty church with that baby on her lap and prayed, "You know how I've messed up my life, God. She's Yours. You may not want me, but please give her hope— hope I don't have for myself."

God answered her prayer. That little girl—now a grown woman— has never *not* known that God loves her and wants her. And, in time, He convinced MaryAnn that He had always loved and wanted her too.

It's honestly one of the most beautiful stories of bravery, redemption, and love I've ever heard. And that amazing woman *is my mom*.

Have you ever wondered what difficulties your parents have had to overcome in life? What they've given up in order to have kids? What sacrifices they're making right now to give you the best life possible?

When you're a teen, it's easy to get so used to the people raising you that you forget they actually have lives. People with names other than Mom and Dad. Men and women with dreams, regrets, interests, and fears. If we can get over ourselves long enough to get to know them, we might just find there's more than meets the eye.

No parent is perfect. But knowing the stuff that has shaped them as people can help you understand where they're coming from. You might have more compassion when they do, say, imply, or command things you find absolutely ludicrous. And I know this sounds crazy, but as you get to know them, you might find out they're pretty cool people you wouldn't mind being friends with someday. At the very least, it might help you treat them like real people—because they are.

Time to Shine

Philippians 2:4 (NLT) says, "Don't look out only for your own interests, but take an interest in others, too." If you want to both get to know your parents better *and* show them you care, start by asking thoughtful questions. It might feel awkward at first, but don't let that stop you! Here are a few to get you started:

- What's your happiest memory?
- How was your relationship with your parents when you were a teen?
- What was your favorite subject in high school? Why?
- Who was your first romantic relationship with?
- How did you meet Mom (or Dad)?
- When you were growing up, what dreams and goals did you have for your life? Which ones have you accomplished?
- How have you changed since you were my age?

Tip #23

If you're standing in a sibling's shadow, move the light source.

Alicia was beautiful and smart, funny and kind. She loved to read, had a bit of sass, and could bake a mean chocolate chip cookie. As the youngest, she was Daddy's girl and her whole family spoiled her. But Alicia didn't feel all that special. In fact, she got the distinct impression that everyone wanted her to be like her older sister. Her sister got perfect grades. Her sister played every sport. Her sister had a Christian boyfriend. Her sister walked on water. And Alicia was just, well, her. It felt like being told to paint a Rembrandt with nothing but a box of crayons at her disposal: impossible.

I know how Alicia felt. Not by personal experience, but because she actually told me so. Alicia is my little sister. And—contrary to the actual state of my moral being—I was the "perfect one" in this tale. (Notice the quotes? That means I wasn't actually perfect. In case there was any confusion.)

According to my sister, when you *think* you're being compared to Mr. or Miss Perfect, you begin to believe the lies. You can practically feel the eyes of everyone watching you, seeing how you'll compare. And by everyone I mean your parents, teachers, coaches, aunts, uncles, youth pastors, grandparents, neighbors, bosses, complete strangers—did I leave anyone out? Maybe you can relate.

At an age when you're trying to figure out who you are and become your own person, living in a sibling's shadow can be extremely discouraging and frustrating. As Alicia taught me, that kind of pressure can make you want to give up, take it out on yourself, or decide to do everything opposite of that brother or sister (even turning away from the "good" in them).

The funny thing about shadows, though, is that they're just an illusion. If you move the light source, the shadow shifts.

Just because your brother or sister *seems* to be doing everything right, that doesn't mean they actually are. Trust me on this one. As a smart, heads-up girl, you'd be wise to move the light around—study your siblings. Watch how they live and learn what you can. How do their choices and beliefs play out? Are they rebelling in secret? If they're making good decisions, learn from those too. Going out of your way to do the opposite out of envy or discouragement will only hurt you.

I love the paraphrase of Galatians 5:26 in *The Message*:

We will not compare ourselves with each other as if one of us were better and another worse. We have far more interesting things to do with our lives. Each of us is an original.

You're an original. Comparison does nothing to improve your life; it only destroys relationships. So be you. And remember that those "perfect" siblings need grace too, because—as Alicia later learned—nobody is faultless, not even this big sis.

Time to Shine

- Do you sometimes feel like you're living with a perfect sibling? Or that your parents have favorites?

- What have you learned by watching your brother or sister?
- If you need help remembering what an original you are, go back to Tip #13 and follow the link to the "Me Quiz" under Time to Shine.

Tip #24

Others' choices will affect you, but they don't have to define you.

When I was seventeen, I met my biological father for the first time.

As a little girl, I used to imagine the day. I'd pull out a square, glass terrarium—a gift he had given my mom—and imagine what he might be like. I was sure he'd be handsome. Definitely kind. Smart too—really smart. He'd probably give me advice about my life, and I'd see which parts of me came from him.

And you know what? I was right.

We met at an upscale restaurant in a big city. As he strode into the lobby, his warm smile instantly put me at ease.

"Someone I know?" he asked, holding out a hand to me.

I shook it, smiling back. "Yes," I said, because I had a feeling that was about to be true.

That night, we talked as if we hadn't spent the entirety of my life apart. He was so genuine in his questions, interested in who I had become and where I wanted to go. During a final, moonlit drive through the city, he gave me advice about choosing a college. He told me to follow my own path, even if it meant disappointing others' expectations. I've never forgotten his words, or the warm night blowing through my hair as we drove. When it was finally time to go, we promised to keep in touch.

His letters, written on company stationery, always made my day as we continued the conversation we had begun. I learned about his work, the two sons he was incredibly proud of, and his love for motorcycles. I eagerly responded each time, updating him on post-graduation plans and telling him I hoped to meet my half brothers someday. It was the happily-ever-after ending I had dreamed about as a girl. Clearly, he wanted to be in my life.

But you know what? It turns out I was wrong.

One day, the letters just stopped coming. I kept trying. I wrote again and again, telling him I understood if he was busy. Apologized if I said anything that offended him. Assured him I wasn't after his money or trying to come between him and his family. I just wanted to have a relationship with him.

I never found out why he changed his mind. Maybe someday I will, but I'm at peace either way. In the silent years since, I've come to understand an important truth that has set my heart free from the rejection: Other people's choices affect me, but they don't define me. I have the choice to let God's love tell me my worth rather than my family wounds.

Abandonment, betrayal, abuse, rejection, divorce—that stuff's gonna hurt like crazy. It might affect the circumstances you find yourself in. But what someone else does can never destroy you or your life unless you let it. Their free will—their power of choice—allows them to make decisions that hurt you. But by God's grace you have the same power, and you can choose to create boundaries, get help, work through your hurts, and forgive. As impossible as it might feel right now, you can live a bright life, regardless of what other people do or say.

I choose to hold on to hope that the story between my biological father and me isn't finished yet. But because I haven't let his choices define me, I'm going to be okay either way, whether I'm right or wrong.

Time to Shine

Have you suffered a significant wound from a family member or close friend? Read this prayer out loud, filling in the blanks with details from your situation.

Father, (name the person) hurt me deeply when they (name what they did). When I think about it, I feel (name the emotions). Show me how to separate myself from their actions. Remind me who I am in You: loved, wanted, and strong. Even when my life feels out of control because of their actions, I know that You work all things together for my good, and my good is ultimately to become more like Christ (Romans 8:28–29). So show me how to become more like Jesus through this. You say that You have good plans for me and my future (Jeremiah 29:11–14). Help me believe it, and to trust You more than my feelings. Amen.

Tips About Health and Beauty

If you ever wonder, *Am I beautiful?*, you're not alone. It's one of the core questions every girl wrestles with! Since having a positive view of your body and taking good care of it go hand in hand, let's explore ways to do both.

Tip #25

Beauty comes in unique versions of lovely. Work with yours.

I once swam in an ocean as clear and bright as liquid aquamarine. The island of Mo'orea sways with salty ocean breezes like Moana's home come to life. Picture the most idyllic tropical paradise, and you get the idea. Swimming with rays and colorful fish feels like you're a guest in another world. The way the sun melted into the sea at dusk took my breath away.

I once climbed a mountain so high, birds flew below me. Half Dome in Yosemite National Park rises like a gray, granite titan. Picture the most epic mountain vista, and you get the idea. Standing at the peak, with a twisting river and green valley stretched out below, feels like you could reach up and touch heaven. The sheer grandeur took my breath away.

I once walked across a desert formation so unique, I can barely think how to describe it. The Wave in Arizona rises and falls in layered stripes like Dr. Seuss made it up. Picture rolling mounds in smooth pastels, and you get the idea. Standing in the middle of symmetrical sandstone feels like you've stepped into a painting. The unique creativity took my breath away.

I once passed through a tropical forest so thick, light filtered down like misty fingers. The Belize jungle smells like a million growing things, ancient and fresh at once. Picture the lushest rainforest, literally humming with life, and you get the idea. Floating down one of its many rivers feels like you died and woke up in Pandora. All that untamed energy took my breath away.

So let me ask you a question: Which of the places I described is beautiful?

A stupid question, right? I bet you'd agree that every single one of them is stunning, in its own, unique way. One location's beauty doesn't disqualify another's. They can all be breathtaking, even though they look nothing alike.

How strange that we can see a truth so plainly in one kind of creation and be completely blind to it in another.

Here's the thing: Human beauty isn't exclusive either. Curly hair is beautiful; so is straight. Dark skin and light skin are equally gorgeous. Wide hips or narrow; tall, short, or in the middle; thick or thin legs; smooth or freckled skin; petite or plump ta-tas—all beautiful!

We often see the characteristics that make us different from others as ugly. I guess we could blame the media and our own sinfulness. It took me a *long* time to realize our differences are actually a big part of the beauty God wove in us. Why would an island envy a mountain, or a jungle wish to be a desert? Once we stop fighting against our design, we can appreciate and work with our uniqueness instead.

There's no one way to be beautiful. Do you agree? If so, act like you believe it, and celebrate *your* unique version of lovely.

Time to Shine

- What are some of the most beautiful places you've ever visited? What made them so?
- Think of three or four people you would describe as good-looking, even though they're quite different from each other. What makes each one attractive?

- This part might be harder, but stick with me. Looking at your features, which ones are different from other people's but could also be described as beautiful?

Tip #26

Stay sun-kissed. The outdoors look good on you.

One time I found myself in a season where I sort of forgot how to live. Nine months of grief, health issues, and moving had sucked me completely dry. I landed in a little coastal town in California—a long-time dream—but still, this usually upbeat girl could barely muster a smile.

About that time, a local high school needed volunteers to chaperone Surf Club. I didn't know how to surf, but apparently just showing up was good enough. That was great because, even though I've always wanted to shred waves like Bethany Hamilton, I hate cold water. With a passion. This ocean was topping out at fifty-five degrees Fahrenheit, only slightly warmer than my refrigerator.

My rear end spent the first few Friday afternoons glued to the sandy beach, watching the groms surf the chilly waves. I made small talk with some of the other adults and counted the minutes till I could go back to my warm car.

Then, one particularly foggy Friday, I sensed God whisper, "Get in the water."

I immediately rattled off a valid list of reasons *not* to get in. "It's *really* cold, God." "I don't even know how to surf." "Aren't there sharks here?" And, most persuasive of all, "I just curled my hair!"

But He wouldn't let it go. After some divine arm twisting, that week I reluctantly bought the thickest wet suit possible, complete with a hood and booties. (I'm not kidding about my aversion to cold water.) The next Surf Club, I borrowed a board and waded into the

Pacific. As the cold water surged around me, something surprising happened. The emotional fog lifted.

The rise and fall of the waves set a new rhythm for my lungs: breathe in, breathe out. The sunlight that danced over the surface of the translucent, blue water put a sparkle in my own eyes. Salty wind blew sea spray across my face, and as I took my first wave, I *smiled*.

Over the coming weeks and months, I spent most Fridays in the water. The sun that brightened my mood also lightened my hair and kissed my skin golden. I grew to love the cold rush of water against my face, the crust of salt in my eyelashes. And, though I'm still no Bethany Hamilton, I did fulfill a lifelong dream and learned how to surf.

I suspect God told me to get in the water because He knew it would be my healing. Getting outside does that. The Japanese call it *shinrin-yoku*, which translates as "forest bathing" and essentially means "to absorb the forest atmosphere." Whether a literal forest, or a park, lake, ocean, or backyard, the idea is to simply pause to notice with all your senses: earthy smells, chirping birds, warm sun on your skin, glistening dew on leaves. As you do, your cortisol (stress) levels go down, your hormones balance, and your endorphins (happy chemicals) go up. Science has proven that taking time in creation and being fully aware of what you're experiencing has incredible benefits to your body and health.

I'd argue that spending time outside also benefits your beauty—it brings your skin a healthy glow, highlights your hair . . . and when you're happy, those unavoidable wrinkles settle as smile lines instead of a perma-frown.

I know, I know—it's too cold (or too hot) out, you don't want to change, it sounds boring, you don't have a car, or you're slammed with homework. I get it. There are always reasons, even valid ones, to put it off. But if you want to live life fully, sometimes you just have to overcome the obstacles, face the uncomfortable, and get in the water.

Time to Shine

Get outside! List three outdoor activities you could reasonably do this week without excuses. If you're having trouble, think small, like a walk around your neighborhood. Now pull out your planner or put a reminder on your phone and set aside time this week to "bathe" in some nature.

Tip #27

Girls are usually blind to their own beauty. Be the exception.

True confession: I once worked with a woman who was so beautiful, I avoided meeting her out of sheer intimidation. Me—a textbook people person. It took me a good two weeks to get over my insecurities and sit next to her during a meeting to introduce myself. Embarrassing, right? What's worse, when I did meet her, she was like the definition of down-to-earth, not to mention kind and fun. Cassy and I became friends, and so— sometime later—I asked her to take a survey for a book on beauty I was writing. I figured there'd be a lot of women who struggled with insecurities about their looks, and I hoped her answers would help balance the negativity. You know, to show that it's possible for someone to be content with how God made her.

Except when Cassy turned in her answers, they didn't balance anything. In fact, of all the women I surveyed, she had the lowest scores on overall satisfaction with her body and the lengthiest descriptions of what she would change about herself—from her overall body frame down to her adorable freckles. (Interestingly, she hated several of the qualities I found most beautiful about her.) I was shocked. How could someone so beautiful feel so ugly?

It's one of the great mysteries of life: Why can't girls see their own beauty?

I know the unbelievable pressure you feel to fit the mold. This Holly-Girl, Insta-Beauty, You-Perfect world we live in presents a very narrow definition of beauty and then suggests we can and should look just like it. And when we glance in the mirror and don't seem to match that definition—well, it's easy to think we're the oddity.

I truly hope you don't worry too much about how you look—that when someone points out your beauty, you're one of the rare, confident girls who can simply smile and say, "Thank you." But if you cringe, change the subject, or shoot down that compliment with the skill of a fighter pilot ("Are you crazy?" "Do you need glasses?"), will you humor me for a minute as we talk about God's master design of the female body?

Beginning in the garden of Eden, God designed man to be drawn to, and captivated by, woman. He made Eve differently from Adam on purpose. Compared to him she had rounder curves, less body hair, leaner muscles, smoother skin texture, different facial symmetry, more delicate bone structure, and an ability to carry new life, for starters. (Now don't do the typical girl thing and start comparing yourself to that list to see if you're "normal," okay? Remember, there are many versions of lovely! We're talking generalities here.) The bottom line? The more I've studied the less-obvious aspects of the female physique, the more I'm convinced that one part of Eve's design was to simply be beautiful.

That means it's part of your design too. Oh, you're also smart, capable, nurturing, strong, and the perfect counterpart to man's masculinity, but don't miss this truth: If you have double X chromosomes, you're a unique kind of beautiful. It's just part of who you are. Sure, you can close your eyes to it and insist God screwed up with you. But if you want to live your brightest life, why not accept that truth and enjoy the beauty hiding right under your nose?

Time to Shine

Sometimes we've been negative toward our body for so long, we genuinely can't see our good and beautiful qualities anymore. If that's the case, try looking through someone else's eyes. What do others tend to compliment you about? Your strong arms or bright smile? How about the shape of your nose or the shade of your eyes?

With those things in mind, write down five of your beautiful traits. If complimenting yourself feels as uncomfortable as pulling on wet jeans, remember: you didn't make your body! It's not prideful to simply recognize the way God designed you.

Tip #28

Speaking of exercise, just *do* something.

As a first-generation Russian immigrant, Valentina sometimes felt out of place around her American classmates. So, a few weeks before her freshman year of high school, she decided to put herself out there and join the volleyball team, hoping to make some friends. Worst case: even if she didn't, at least she'd get out of the house and have something to do.

On the first day of tryouts, her mom dropped her off at the school. Since it was still summer break, the grounds were pretty empty. Worried that maybe she had gotten the time or day wrong, she wandered around campus a bit, searching for anyone else in gym shorts and tennis shoes. Eventually, she spotted a group of athletic-looking students gathered on the lawn. Relieved, she slipped into their circle and started following the girl leading them in stretches.

When they finished, the coach announced they'd take a little warm-up run to the red church and back. Valentina didn't see any red church, but she fell in line with the group as they jogged off down the road.

Eight miles later, they returned to the school, sweaty and out of breath. Turns out Valentina had accidentally joined the cross-country team. She was too embarrassed to tell anyone, so she stuck with it the entire season. And the next. And the *next*. She ran cross-country all four years of high school. Never did try out for volleyball.

While I hope you get to choose on purpose (grin), *what* you do for exercise isn't nearly as important as just getting your body moving. The benefits are too amazing to skip. Exercise:

- builds endurance and muscle strength, which in turn give you more energy.
- helps strengthen and maintain your bones, muscles, and joints. Fewer injuries? Yes, please.
- promotes better posture, which causes others to see you as more confident and capable.
- contributes to a healthy body (which can outwardly look different for everyone) and lowers your risk of just about every major disease.
- releases endorphins (aka "happy hormones"), which reduce stress, anxiety, and depression.
- literally makes you feel better about your body, even before there's a hint of visible change.

Keeping your body moving helps you enjoy life two ways. First, it keeps your body in top shape so it can physically handle the things you want to do. Second, when done right, exercise can be a lot of fun, especially when you "play" with friends.

Formal sports teams have become a pretty big part of being an American teen, but if that's not your thing, don't write off exercise completely. You could walk, bike, run, dance, swim, skate, join a gym, or get a job that keeps you moving. The possibilities are as endless as the benefits. How you move is up to you, as long as you do something.

Time to Shine

Business, homework, and our screens can make it hard to find time to exercise. Though once we get active, we're always glad we did, right? Focusing on the rewards, write down three ways you can fit exercise into your routine this week. If you can commit to a full workout, great! If not, think simple, like walking around your school campus during lunch.

1. _____
_____

2. _____
_____

3. _____
_____

Tip #29

You only get one body. Take care of it.

One of my mom's famously endearing quirks was her willingness to drive ridiculous distances for just a few minutes with those she loved. So I wasn't *completely* shocked when she asked if my little sister and I wanted to go to her hometown for her niece's wedding. Never mind that Sheboygan, Wisconsin, was 2,124 miles away; she assured me we could make it there and back in three days so I wouldn't miss my big volleyball game. She sweetened the deal by promising I could put my newly acquired driver's license to use. Done. We packed my little sis and no small arsenal of snacks into the back seat and hit the road.

We cruised from sun-swept California to the deserts of Nevada, past vivid red hills in Utah and autumn-gold aspen forests in Colorado. And when it got dark, Mom somehow stayed awake through the flat farmland of Nebraska and Iowa, until we finally crossed into the glorious land of cheese curds and Green Bay Packers the next day.

Amazingly, we made it to the wedding in just under thirty-six hours. We cried, we cheered, we threw rice. Then we loaded back into the car and onto the open road.

Thirty-six hours sounded a lot longer on the return trip. To make matters worse, a few states in, our trusty car started sounding funny. Nothing too alarming, though, so we just kept driving. Then we overheated in Utah. Thirty minutes and a bottle of coolant later, we were back on the interstate. But it happened again in Nevada. By the time we crossed the California state line, Mom knew something was seriously wrong.

In my memory, that car limped and sputtered its way into our driveway, then sighed a final goodbye before releasing its spirit to the automotive afterlife in a pillar of steam. It may or may not have been that dramatic in real time, but one fact was crystal clear: our 72-hour, 4,248-mile road trip had run the engine into the ground.

We expected that car to just keep chuggin' along, no matter how hard we pushed it. But it only had so much to give before it couldn't take any more.

God has given you a body to take you places in life—to hike, run, dance, swim, play, and accomplish. If you treat it right, it'll serve you well. If you run it into the ground, you'll be the one to suffer.

I know sometimes it feels like you have no choice but to be hard on your body. You've got more to do than you can get done, a lot of stress to manage. You don't have time to eat healthy, sleep well, or exercise. But your body keeps score. No, you might not feel it today or tomorrow. Across the miles of your life, though? Not taking care of yourself will take a toll, including how it will affect your mind and emotions.[1]

You'll only be able to go as far as your body will take you. If you want to live extraordinarily in the second, third, and even fourth quarters of life, make sure your "vehicle" stays up to the task. Take care of it. If you treat it well, your healthy body and mind will go the distance with you.

---

1. Brain function is part of your physical body, and remember, how you think influences how you feel.

Time to Shine

Learning to treat your body well will take more than reading this quick tip. To educate yourself, you'll have to get curious about how your body works and the best ways to care for it. Why not start today? For each category below, do a little research. Read an article, ask an expert, or watch a video, then write down a few bits of interesting or helpful advice. (Sidenote: this is a good time to mention that learning which "experts" to trust is another important life skill!)

Exercise:_____

_____

Mental Clarity:_____

_____

Flexibility:_____

_____

Food: _____

_____

Sleep:_____

_____

Tip #30

Eat for fuel more often than pleasure. Your body will thank you.

Jordan Rubin was a pretty healthy nineteen-year-old when he started his freshman year at Florida State University. But over the course of that year, his health completely dive-bombed. It started with painful digestive issues that quickly progressed to feeling nauseous all the time. Before long, he had lost eighty pounds and was in and out of the hospital. His body got so weak and emaciated that he had to use a wheelchair. Answers were hard to come by. Eventually, he was diagnosed with Crohn's disease, but that seemed to be just the tip of the iceberg. One doctor told him it was the worst case of Crohn's he had ever seen and, sadly, he didn't expect Jordan to live much longer.

Jordan and his parents searched the world for help and prayed for a miracle. After trying seventy different therapies, his quest to live eventually led him to a unique nutritionist. This man taught him that if he wanted to be healthy, he had to follow "God's health plan."

Studying Bible passages about living a healthy lifestyle, Jordan began eating foods the way God originally made them, including lots of fruits and vegetables, whole grains, and fermented dairy. Two years of being seriously ill had taken a toll on his body and mind, but within *forty days*, this new way of eating began a drastic transformation.

Over the next year, Jordan completely regained his health—not a single disease remained. All by changing the food he put into his body.

I first heard Jordan's story when I reviewed his book *The Maker's Diet* for a work assignment. My mind was blown. How had I made it to my midtwenties without understanding the link between what I ate and how I felt? Growing up on the standard American diet (ironically, SAD for short), I guess I thought it was normal to feel tired, moody, and bloated and struggle to keep off the extra pounds. Turns out, my love for pizza and sweet tea wasn't doing me any favors! Jordan's experience revolutionized my own health, and launched a lifelong curiosity to learn which foods will help my body function at its best and find its natural ideal weight.[1]

If your body's like a vehicle that will take you the places you want to go in life (remember Tip #29?), then what you eat is literally the fuel that powers the car. Do you know what happens when you put the wrong type of gas in a vehicle? Say, unleaded in a diesel? You literally break the engine! Your body works similarly. It needs the right kind of fuel to power strong.

God gave us taste buds for a reason. He wanted us to enjoy the explosion of flavors He created in this world—the sheer ecstasy of a perfectly sweet blueberry, creamy avocado, or savory vanilla bean. The ability to enjoy food is a divine gift. But like all gifts, focusing too much on it can backfire on us. Humans have messed with the way God made food, adding salt, sugar, and chemicals to amplify the pleasure. In the process, we've created cuisine that tastes better but can make our bodies run worse.

Of course, pleasure isn't all bad! Enjoy the finer tastes in this world—in balance. Thank God for the gift of ice cream. Just remember that if you focus on eating foods that will fuel your body best,

---

1. I don't follow *The Maker's Diet*, or any other diet, exclusively. I share this story to highlight the powerful relationship between food and our health, not as an endorsement of any one way of eating.

you'll reap all kinds of rewards: clearer skin, balanced hormones, higher energy, fewer mood swings, better sports performance, and a healthier future (to name a few). That sounds like a recipe for a great life to me.

Time to Shine

Write down a list of your favorite unprocessed foods that God created for you to enjoy *and* that fuel your body well. (Think a fresh apple instead of packaged, sweetened applesauce, or a handful of almonds instead of chips.)

1. _____

2. _____

3. _____

4. _____

5. _____

How do you feel when you eat these foods?

Tip #31

If you want to be happier about you, slow the media drip.

A few weeks ago, I got asked to film a short promo video for an awesome nonprofit. Not only was I excited about the opportunity to spread the word about a cause I believe in, I was just plain honored that they considered me talented enough for the role. And, if I'm being honest, I was feeling pretty good about myself. I mean, they wouldn't have picked me if I was *unpleasant* to look at, right?

Because of the location of the shoot—a sweeping California coastline—I figured a new outfit was in order. Something relaxed chic (Cali's signature style). I got to work browsing three of my favorite online retailers looking for the perfect I-care-but-don't-care top. You know how these things go, right? Four-point-three hours later, I had sifted through approximately 752 images and was no closer to finding the perfect shirt.

What I *did* find as I browsed the flood of picture-perfect models, however, was that my waist could be a tad bit slimmer. My nose? It sticks out a good deal too far. And those *pores*—when did they decide to resemble sinkholes? Little creases suddenly appeared, right there at the corner of my mouth. I concluded it was possible I would need actual plastic surgery before I could agree to be on camera.

In a matter of a few hours, I went from feeling confident to absolutely convinced I wasn't nearly pretty enough.

I gave up on finding a shirt. And it took a fair amount of telling my thoughts who's boss to get out of my head enough to show up and smile the day of the shoot.

The film crew was very kind—*over-the-top* encouraging. As if sensing my sudden insecurity, the producer assured me multiple times, "You're perfect for this," and "You look great." The funniest irony is that I'm only on-screen nine-point-five seconds in the finished video. And, merciful Jesus, the golden hour light coats the coast so beautifully, you can't see a single pore on my nose. The nonprofit's amazing work is the highlight, as it should be.

I wish I could say this was the only time an internet search (or social media scroll) sent me into a mini body-image spiral. But my momma taught me not to tell lies. I've come a long way since my disordered eating days; I even wrote a whole book about understanding our true beauty as girls. Still, I'm not immune to letting images of "perfection" distort my view, any more than you might be. I know that to be a happier, more confident version of me, I have to slow the IV drip of media I consume. Sometimes I have to pull the needle out of my arm altogether.

Obviously, the answer isn't to avoid *all* outside influences. That's unrealistic. I mean, at some point I will have to buy another shirt. But we can take a look at our hearts every so often, and ask God to show us whether all those photos and videos we see of a narrow type of beauty influence us more than we realize. We want to live free from all that.

If you're struggling to find the beauty in you, try distancing yourself from your usual diet of media for a bit. That might look like screen time limits, deleting some apps, unsubscribing from certain channels, or even a media fast. You don't have anything to lose by giving it a shot, and you just might find a happier, more confident version of you waiting on the other side.

Time to Shine

- Would you say that the things you watch and look at affect your body image?
- If you answered yes, give some specific examples of what impacts your mood about yourself.
- What's one way you can cut back on the amount of "perfection" you consume today?

Tip #32

The fewer mirrors you see, the more you'll see the real you.

Midway through high school, some family friends were redecorating their house and asked if we could use some furniture. Let's just say my family was less likely to be shopping at Pottery Barn than behind a *real* barn, so the prospect of free furniture was an easy yes. It wasn't fancy stuff, but I still remember being pretty excited the day we hauled that twin bed frame and desk up the narrow stairs into my second-story bedroom.

Not long after, they called again, asking if I had room for a mirror. I thought that was a strange thing to ask, since my room was pretty average-size and mirrors don't generally take up that much space. Figuring they were just being polite, I gladly accepted.

When the mirror arrived, though, all became clear. The thing was gargantuan. Like nearly floor-to-ceiling and four feet wide. Wide-eyed, but not wanting to be rude, I thanked them profusely and we somehow maneuvered it up the stairs and into my room.

I was now the owner of a mirror roughly the size of a small car. Since it took up a third of my wall space, I tried to make it blend in, decorating the border with magazine clippings and a few Bible verses.

The giant mirror wouldn't have been an issue, except, as the days passed, I kept *looking at it*. I didn't mean to, but it was so big I could see myself from nearly any corner of the room. My reflection attracted my attention worse than Jake in chemistry class. And each time I stopped to look closer, I noticed more things I had been oblivious to before. My hips were . . . wider than I thought. That mole on my face—had it always been there? Why was my hair limper than a wet noodle? Was I too tall? No, not tall enough. Ugh!

Picking apart what I saw in my giant mirror quickly became a giant problem. All that self-reflection tanked my self-image. By the time I realized what was happening, a lot of damage had been done.

Mirrors themselves aren't necessarily evil, and I'm not suggesting you should never look in one. How else would you see the food stuck between your teeth? But if you struggle to see your true beauty, might I suggest you'll view it more clearly the less time you spend in front of a mirror? (Especially one of the giant variety.) I've found that the fewer I have in plain sight, the better I actually see.

If you're math savvy, the equation might read:

$$x * -1 = \text{confidence level}$$

$$\text{if}$$

$$x = \text{number of mirrors}$$

So today I'm down to one mirror above my bathroom sink, a portable full-length stored in the closet, and a tabletop makeup mirror aimed at the wall when not in use. And you know what? I'm a much happier person.

If you, too, want the freedom of self-forgetfulness, try downsizing the number of mirrors in your life. It's a simple, practical hack guaranteed to improve your confidence. If you do get rid of some, though, do me a favor and don't offer them to me.

Time to Shine

Take inventory of how many mirrors you currently have access to every day (your room, house, locker, backpack, etc.). Evaluate which ones you could move, cover, or get rid of altogether to make it easier to avoid critiquing yourself.

Tip #33

"Improving" your beauty always comes at a cost. Decide what's worth paying.

Like most women across cultures and throughout history, Panya felt a ton of pressure to be considered beautiful by the people around her. In her culture, light skin was in. At that time in Thailand, the darker your skin, the higher the chance you made a low-class living outdoors in the rice paddies. If you wanted to look wealthier, you had to look whiter.

As a local singer, the pressure to achieve high-class beauty weighed on Panya. So when one of her friends told her about a skin-lightening cream sold at the local open-air market, she was all in. She eagerly applied the cream to her face and arms, anticipating a transformation into fair loveliness.

At first, the magic lotion seemed to work perfectly. Her skin started lightening almost immediately. After a while, she noticed layers of her skin began peeling off. *Not to worry,* she thought, *it's just part of the process. The price of beauty.* So she continued applying it each morning. Then one day, while she had to spend some time in the sun, her skin felt like it was on fire. Whatever chemicals laced the cream literally burned her skin, causing terrible damage. The permanent scars to her face, arms, and hands made her skin a mottled blend of dark and light. She was embarrassed to go out in public, lost her job as a singer, and her husband left her. What started as a quest to be more beautiful cost her much more than she expected.[1]

---

1. *Jessica Simpson's The Price of Beauty,* VH1, episode 101, first aired March 12, 2010.

Over the years I've come to learn there's *always* a cost to improving our appearance. No, the price isn't always as steep as what Panya paid, but at the same time, it's often more than we realize. Before we talk about the cost, consider some of the stuff we American girls are known to do in the twenty-first century for the sake of beauty:

- Apply makeup
- Change hair color
- Wear a bra
- Remove hair from legs, arms, or other body parts
- Thread or glue on fake eyelashes
- Weave in hair extensions
- Paint nails or get acrylics
- Wear jewelry
- Straighten or curl hair
- Get plastic surgery or injections
- Use an acne cream
- Apply a facial
- Wear braces
- Use a filter to touch up photos or videos

Whether we plump, apply, shave, cut, pierce, thin, or wax, it's going to cost something. Obviously, there's a monetary cost. "Beauty" has become a $500 billion industry![2] But what about a time cost? What if it causes us to be more preoccupied with

---

2. Bethany Baron, "Beauty has blown up to be a $532 billion industry—and analysts say that these 4 trends will make it even bigger." *Business Insider,* July 9, 2019. https://www .businessinsider.com/beauty-multibillion-industry-trends-future-2019-7?op=1 , accessed October 23, 2023.

ourselves, costing us our self-worth? And if we're perpetuating a certain standard of perfection, could there be a cost to others?

On the flip side, some routines can bring joy, bump up our confidence, and highlight the beauty God gives us. For example, applying makeup and curating outfits can be a form of artistic expression. One friend gets her nails done every month just to spend quality time with her mom.

So saying it's never worth any cost to improve your beauty isn't true. Saying it's always worth any cost also isn't true. That means we have to wrestle with some tension and decide for ourselves what's worth it, based on our culture, faith, self-respect, and knowledge.

As with everything in life, I believe God cares most about our hearts here. It can bring Him glory when we enjoy and cultivate the beauty He has given us. But He also wants us to live free from a beauty obsession. So "don't lose sight of common sense and discernment. Hang on to them, for . . . they are like jewels on a necklace" (Proverbs 3:21–22, NLT).

As a woman who wants to be beautiful, I know my weaknesses. If I'm not careful, I'll easily spend too much on that face mask promising glass skin, or take so long getting ready in the morning that I run out of time to read my Bible. That's why when I'm considering whether a new beauty product or process is worth the cost to me, I try to ask myself three questions:

- What's my motivation?
- What's the real cost?
- Is the price worth it?

If you want to avoid unexpected, unreasonable costs of beauty, learn to ask yourself those questions too. And coming to appreciate how beautiful you *already* are will also help you decide what's wise to pay.

Time to Shine

Practice evaluating the cost of the products you use and things you do to look more beautiful. Write down three to five examples from your personal routine. For each item, ask: What's my motivation? What's the real cost? Is the price worth it?

1. _____

   Motivation: _____

   Real cost: _____

   Worth it? _____

2. _____

   Motivation: _____

   Real cost: _____

   Worth it? _____

3. _____

   Motivation: _____

   Real cost: _____

   Worth it? _____

Tip #34

You're not getting any younger. Plan to age well.

"An old lady what?" I asked, genuinely confused.

"An old lady *file*," she repeated.

I had just met Jean at an event in Colorado, where I had been asked to share about a book I had written for teen girls. Jean was invited to speak to the opposite end of the age spectrum about living the final years well.

"Tell me more," I said with a smile, curiosity piquing my interest. Jean might have been more than twice my age, but her confident poise and kind smile drew me in. I had a feeling her pillowy gray hair came with hard-won wisdom, and I wanted to hear it.

"Well," she said, "when I was younger, I was afraid of getting old. So I started collecting articles, snippets, Scriptures, and the like about aging with purpose. It has become quite a collection!"

She went on to explain that while society focuses on—even idolizes—the beauty of youth, since God designed us to get old, she decided He must have had His reasons. Her old lady file acted like a vision board when she was in her forties, fifties, and sixties, inspiring her to believe her best years were *still* up ahead—both for her body and her soul. And judging by the woman in front of me, it had worked! She was full of life and loveliness.

"Old age comes for us all," she said with a laugh. "If you don't want to dread the prospect, I suggest rethinking age in your earlier years."

And so I have.

Shortly after meeting Jean Fleming, I started my own old lady file. Mine's not an actual paper folder, but I have a spot on my computer where I bookmark and save geriatric gems. It holds inspiring stories about women making their lives count in the final quarter of life, places I want to see, people I could serve, tips for keeping my body strong, and photos of silver-haired beauties with smile lines in all the right places.

Maybe you haven't given much thought to your thirties, let alone your final decades on earth. "Old" is what happens to *other people,* right? People like your grandparents, with their soft, wrinkled faces and wobbly handwriting. It's pretty normal to view old age as a vague blur of gray hair, knitting needles, and Jell-O.

But we're not after "normal," are we? Even in your teens and twenties, Jean's advice is really, *really* smart. Think about it: If your definition of beauty only includes young, smooth skin, then when you look in the mirror to discover that first wrinkle or gray hair, how are you going to feel? Yeah, *not* beautiful! Then you might be tempted to wallow in self-doubt or spend a lot of money on products or procedures to "fix" the signs of aging. Or if you're convinced that life after thirty contains nothing but work and drudgery, that could become a self-fulfilling prophecy.

Instead, if you cast a vision for life getting better and brighter with age—of beauty deepening instead of fading and of finding new opportunities in each decade—then you'll march toward the future with some sass. Look for and celebrate the unique beauty of aging people now, and when it's your turn you'll still see how lovely you are, no matter how old you get.

Time to Shine

You're never too young to start an old lady file! Find a place to collect photos, stories, and other inspiring snippets of women looking fabulous and living life well in their thirties, forties, and beyond.

Tips About Faith

There's a reason one of Jesus's names is Light of the World. His presence in our lives can turn darkness into summertime sun. If you want to live a bright life—one full of purpose, joy, and hope—these tips will help you grow in your faith as you get to know God better.

Tip #35

Like Siri, God doesn't run out of forgiveness.

I'm confident enough in my womanhood to admit this to you: I'm directionally challenged. I'm smart, witty, capable, and strong, but give me a map and a compass and I will still get myself as lost as a kid in a corn maze.

It's so frustrating to think you're going the right way only to find out you're not. That's why Siri and I have a special bond. She directs and I follow, because I will end up in the wrong parts of town if left to myself. I trust her lead, because she magically knows where she's going and how to get me there. (Except for that one time she led me to the middle of a dirt field in Berthoud, Colorado. No joke. But when she found a random Chipotle on the way home, all was forgiven.)

This might sound crazy, but since she has been a trustworthy guide, I feel a wash of guilt when I don't listen to her. Like, if she says, "At the next intersection, make a U-turn," and I don't do it, I feel like I'm dissing a faithful friend. Even if I'm just making a quick detour for gas, or have to go around a roadblock, I find myself apologizing. To my phone. "I'm sorry, Siri. I just have to . . ."

And if I ignore too many commands in a row, I get worried she's going to be mad at me or something. As if she'll get so fed up with me ignoring her advice that she'll switch into some snarky voice function and bark, "Well, if you're so smart, missy, get your own directionally challenged butt home!"

I fear the imagined wrath of inanimate AI technology. A strange neurosis, I know. Even stranger, I treat God that way sometimes too.

Since He's a trustworthy guide, I worry that if I ignore His directions too long, He'll get fed up with my stupid choices, switch into a booming God voice, and bellow, "Well, if you think you're so smart, Jessie, why don't you figure out life on your own? I'm outta here."

It's good to feel guilty when I ignore His directions and drive straight toward sin. But once I course-correct, admitting I was wrong and asking God to forgive my stupid stubbornness, I don't have to worry that God will get tired of my apologies and give up on me. Thinking God will run out of forgiveness is as ridiculous as thinking Siri will stop giving me directions. Neither God nor Siri are going to react like an impatient human would, because that's just not their nature.

I can't completely understand God's generous forgiveness because it's so "other." It doesn't make sense to this puny brain of mine. But the Bible tells me He really does forgive me when I repent—even my biggest mess-ups, even the sins I've committed over and over again, even when I knew better (see 1 John 1:9, Isaiah 1:18, Psalm 103:12, 2 Corinthians 5:18–19, Romans 8:1, and more).

The key to accepting God's illogical forgiveness is remembering that He isn't like us. Hopefully, that grace will inspire us to listen the first time He gives us directions!

Time to Shine

- Do you have a hard time believing that God really forgives you when you repent from your biggest mess-ups, or sins you've committed too many times to count?
- How might pride be at play when we have a hard time accepting God's forgiveness for something we "knew better" than to do?

- Read these verses and write any especially meaningful words or verses in your journal: 1 John 1:9, Isaiah 1:18, Psalm 103:12, 2 Corinthians 5:18–19, and Romans 8:1.

Tip #36

Long for life-ever-after with Jesus.

I stood at the place where the Atlantic Ocean kissed the rough sand of a Cuban beach. The sun's last rays turned clouds into tangerine cotton candy. Salty wind pulled at the tops of waves and played with stray strands of my hair. I closed my eyes and took a deep breath—tried to draw in the beauty of it, hoping it would fill the space inside that felt so . . . missing. It didn't work. When I opened my eyes, the swaying ocean, though magical, only reminded me of his stormy blues.

I longed for him so much, it hurt.

It had been almost three months since I left home to study in Central America; three months since Paul's presence was tangible, not just a thought or memory. I couldn't seem to go an hour without thinking about him, dreaming about "us," counting down the minutes until I'd see him again. We planned to get engaged and married soon, so I was secure in his love despite thousands of miles between us. But that didn't stop the longing. Nope. Just made it worse.

When I was a kid, I remember my mom talking about how much she longed for Jesus to come back. I knew her life had been pretty rough, and the world hadn't stopped getting crazier, so I figured she was anxious for heaven so the pain and suffering would end. But as I've walked longer on this earth, hand in hand with Jesus, I think I had it wrong. She wasn't so much longing for Jesus to restore the earth; she was anxious to be restored to *Him*.

The longer we follow Jesus, the more we'll long for life-ever-after with Him.

If you've put your faith in Christ, you have a heavenly fiancé to anticipate. There's a wedding in your future, because He has promised to come for His bride—us, the church. In Revelation, we get a glimpse of that future, happy day:

> The time has come for the wedding feast of the Lamb, and his bride has prepared herself. She has been given the finest of pure white linen to wear. . . . Blessed are those who are invited to the wedding feast of the Lamb. (Revelation 19:7–9, NLT)

Those verses take me back to all the feelings on that Cuban beach. We've had a taste of Jesus in this life, but the best—our complete union—is yet to come. We are going to be with Him—physically *with Him!* We know we are going to be reunited, so we can live confident in His love today.

During the months I was in Central America, far away from the man I loved, the knowledge that we'd be together again changed everything. As much as I enjoyed the countries where I studied, I always knew I was just passing through—my "home" was with Paul. It steadied my affections as well. I met some really great guys along the way, but I was never tempted to think of any of them as more than friends. And being apart also revealed what my heart truly wanted. I found that, as much as I loved to travel and explore, the exotic locations fell flat without Paul there to share them with.

Knowing we'll be together with Jesus in person someday changes everything too. It reminds us that we're just passing through this world, which in turn affects what we do with our time, abilities, money, and more. It can also steady our affections. When we know we're going to be united with perfection someday, it makes it easier to embrace singleness, or say no to the guy we know isn't best for us. And ultimately, being apart reveals what our hearts want: Is it truly Christ and His kingdom? Or are we so focused on this world that we hardly give our "someday" with Jesus a second thought?

Let's become the soon-to-be bride that can't seem to go more than an hour without thinking about Him, dreaming about "us," and counting down the minutes until our Groom takes us into His arms for eternity.

Time to Shine

Write a love note to Jesus. Tell Him a few things you admire about Him, how grateful you are to be His, and why you're anxious to be with Him in person someday. You don't have to make it weird or flowery—just be yourself.

Tip #37

Ask for miracles. Trust God's answers.

Yosemite glittered under a blanket of fresh snow, fitting for the start of an equally fresh year. It was New Year's Day, and Paul and I were celebrating our engagement anniversary at the place where he proposed. We had spent the day crisscrossing the quiet valley, looking for the perfect angles for Paul to snap photos. Our search took us from one end of Yosemite to the other: under the shadow of towering El Capitan, along the winding King's River, between bare trees shivering in cold mountain air, to a tiny church dripping with age and icicles. As the shadows grew longer and our stomachs began complaining, we stopped at Curry Village for a snack. That's when Paul noticed something important was missing from his ring finger.

Our stomachs dropped. We started by upending the car, digging under seats and between cushions. No luck. I think we lost 90 percent of our hope at that point. Finding a silver wedding ring in snow-covered Yosemite Valley was about as close as you can come to the cliché "finding a needle in a haystack." But we reluctantly retraced our steps, scanning trails and bridges as we backtracked. No surprise, we didn't find it.

As we followed the road out of Yosemite, Paul asked if he could stop for one last picture at the first place we had visited that morning. He ran ahead, eager to catch the late-afternoon sun illuminating stories-high icicles where waterfalls should be. I took my time along the trail, the pad of my boots against soft snow the only sound. Pausing to breathe in the crisp air, I looked at the sky and prayed, "Lord, I know You know where Paul's ring is. And if You'd show us, we'll always remember every January first that You're a God who does miracles." When I glanced down at my feet, there in the snow—making a perfect silver circle—was Paul's ring.

A few years later, Paul and I were backpacking in the Sierra Nevada mountains. After hiking all day, we set up camp near a glassy lake and made some freeze-dried fried rice for dinner. That's when Paul noticed something important was missing from his ring finger. *Again.*

Our stomachs dropped. How could he lose it a second time? We had zero hope we'd find it. We had covered eight miles that day, and I was too embarrassed to ask God for a second miracle for the same blasted ring. But we halfheartedly searched the campsite and the surrounding area. Not surprising, no luck.

Paul took his camera to hike a nearby ridge for the sunset. I opted to get into my warm sleeping bag instead. As I made my way into the tent, I finally prayed, "God, I'm so embarrassed that we lost it again. We should have gotten that ring resized the first time. It's totally our fault. But I know You know where it is, and You, obviously, *can* do miracles, so . . . I mean . . . we'd really appreciate it if You'd help us find it."

I shimmied into my sleeping bag, and as I pulled it up to my chest—I kid you not—there on top of my bag was that missing silver ring.

A few years later Paul and I were making a funny video for a camp where we worked. Basically, I was supposed to pretend to punch a life-sized hockey puck in someone's front yard. (Don't ask.) During one of the many takes, my wedding ring must have made an exit from my finger. That's my best guess, anyway, because that afternoon I noticed it was missing. After having Paul's ring miraculously returned not once, but twice, this time I had a bit of hope that God would return it. I mean, a front lawn wasn't nearly as daunting as Yosemite in snow, or an entire *mountain*. For God, this was child's play. Plus, mine was worth more money than Paul's. Surely that counted for something.

We searched the grass on our hands and knees four times, inspected the gutters, and combed through the house for good measure. But we never did find my wedding ring.

I've come to believe these stories are three parts to one whole truth. God hears our prayers and still does miracles today. I learned that firsthand when He returned Paul's ring on New Year's Day. When God returned the ring a second time, He proved He doesn't run out of answers (or grace!), even when we've received mercy before. We can keep asking, even when we're embarrassed, because God enjoys giving us good gifts (see Matthew 7:11). That said, God didn't miraculously return my own ring. I learned He doesn't always say yes, but that doesn't mean He hasn't heard or isn't able. That was important to know later in life, when He said no to a job I really wanted, or to healing my mom from cancer.

So when you need a miracle, ask. You can trust He'll say yes whenever He can, He'll say no when it contradicts some higher purpose you can't see today, and He's a good God either way.

Time to Shine

- Whether you've personally experienced a miracle or not, do you believe God still does them sometimes?
- Have you ever asked God to come through on something, but He said no (or, at least, it seemed like He did)?
- Do you need a God-sized answer to prayer today? Ask Him for a miracle. Watch for it. Then trust His answer.

Tip #38

Spend time with God, and His way will have a way of getting into you.

Once I took a year-round job at a Christian camp deep in the mountains. Living and working in such a remote location made for some unique adventures. I was smack-dab in the middle of a huge national park. No Starbucks, no mall, and no cell coverage. As in, I had to drive almost two hours to get to Target. Or *anywhere*. I had officially relocated to the boondocks.

After several months of culture shock, I got used to taking a giant cooler with me "down the hill" for grocery shopping; turning off my cell phone for a week or more at a time; and living, working, and going to church with the same small group of people. I amassed my share of bear stories, power outages, and waist-high snowstorms. I learned how to forage for gooseberries and which pine trees smelled strangely of vanilla. You could call me a regular mountain woman.

While I expected to enjoy the pretty scenery, I didn't anticipate how much the mountains would *get into me*. When you spend weeks, months, and years away from freeway traffic, smog, sirens, hustle, fast food, and endless distractions, your soul breathes in a way you didn't realize it was suffocating. When twelve-thousand-foot mountains fill your backyard, thunderstorms become summer afternoon entertainment, and the only nighttime lights are more stars than you knew existed, God feels ever-present.

I didn't realize how much I had changed until I left.

When I said farewell to the Sierras and once again made my

home in a "big city," I flopped around like a fish out of water—like my soul was gasping for breath. My time in the mountains had transformed me. Slowly. Consistently. *Completely.*

I recently pulled my old journals from a dusty box in my shed for some research. Thumbing through the story of my life—from ten years old to today—I realized something for the first time. In my tweens and teens, between the sunny days my life was also noisy, sprinkled with drama, marked by some poor choices, and filled with questions. But all those years I loved God and I spent time getting to know Him. Year after year, I carved out moments for the two of us, to read His words to me and write out my prayers to Him. Sometimes an hour; sometimes a few minutes. Sometimes daily, sometimes with year-long gaps. But I stuck with it. And something happens when we spend time with Him—when we read the Bible, worship, pray, and listen for His voice. His presence has a way of *getting into* us. Transforming us. Slowly. Consistently. *Completely.*

Now I'm not the same person who wrote, "Today for my birthday party, we went roller skating," on the top line in my first peach-colored diary with the gold lock. In the decades since writing that sentence, God's Spirit has been working between every line I've written—convicting, teaching, making broken parts of me beautiful. Reading through all those years of life reminded me how far I've come.

That's why I take time to just "be" with God. (One of the reasons, anyway.) It's also why I've made church a priority, hang out with other believers, and find books by authors who know God the way I want to—because they have God's Spirit in them too and He often speaks to me through their wisdom and experiences. Someday, when I pull out even more journals from a dusty box in my shed and I look back over the story of my life yet to come, I want to see that He continued to change me. I want to celebrate the ways my soul learned to walk in step with His Spirit, what ugly parts of me He'll help me grow past. I want to read about the ways God comes through for me in the highs and lows ahead.

If you want to live your brightest life, don't underestimate how spending time with Jesus (and His true followers!) will transform you. It may seem like a waste of time today. You may wonder if it's doing any good at all. But if you keep at it, I promise God's words, presence, and character will change you, a bit like spending years in a remote mountain town.

Time to Shine

Take some time to think about how far you've come in your life. If you keep a journal, read over some of your past entries. If you don't have a written record, try to think back to "you" from five years ago—your interests, attitudes, fears, who you liked, etc. How have you changed for the better? Celebrate who you've become! Ask God to keep changing you as you spend time with Him.

Tip #39

Pride takes many forms. None of them bring you closer to God.

I needed some wheels. I still had four days left on the island of Mo'orea and had seen everything I could on my rented bicycle. I heard the must-see snorkeling spot was twenty-one kilometers away. Definitely farther than I could walk. Rental car? Too expensive for my budget. My singular attempt at hitchhiking had been hilariously difficult, so I ruled that out too.

For better or worse, I'm the kind of girl who lives by the adage *where there's a will, there's a way.* I remembered seeing some European-style scooters zipping around. What about one of those? After finding Mo'orea Scooter online, the price was reasonable, so I reserved one and faced hitchhiking a second time to get to the lot.

The "lot" consisted of a repurposed shipping container. The man behind the counter spoke mostly French—of which I know none—but with some pointing and smiling I managed to communicate that I was there to pick up one of the cute little scooters inside.

After fitting me with a helmet, he handed me some paperwork. In broken English he asked, "You know to drive scooter, yes?"

Let me pause here to say that there are very few rules governing scooter rental in Mo'orea. Mostly you just have to know how to drive one. I didn't *technically* fit that description, but I had seen lots of tourists driving them. Average tourists. Old tourists. I figured if *they* could drive a scooter around, surely I—capable, smart, and oh-so-humble Jessie—could figure it out, no problem. How hard could it be? So when he asked, I decided that knowing *how* to drive a scooter and knowing I could *learn* to drive a scooter were basically the same thing.

"Yep," I replied, nodding.

If he suspected my bluff, he didn't let on.

"Okay, small refresher," he began, and gave me the standard speech-slash-charades about the brake and gas levers, how to lock it up, and the location of the turn signals.

"And remind me," I said, "how do you turn it on?"

He looked at me a little sideways, but kindly showed me how to turn the key while holding the brake. Then he sent me on my way.

I hopped on that Peugeot Tweet 50 like I was made for it, rolled up the kickstand, and took a deep breath. My first maneuver would be making a left-hand turn onto a moderately busy, two-lane highway right across from a crosswalk where a dozen or so people were waiting. *No problem, Jess. You've got this.*

I revved the gas and the scooter lurched forward, fast. Too fast. Adrenaline shot through me as I sped across the first lane of traffic—I was headed straight for the crowd! *Turn, Jess, turn!* I yelled at myself, yanking the handlebar, but the scooter didn't seem to be listening. Why wasn't it turning? At the last moment, the crowd's eyes widening in fear, I dropped my left foot to the pavement, which forced my body to lean hard left. The scooter swerved left too, narrowly missing the crowd *and* a metal pole.

I learned two important lessons that day. One, when on a scooter, you have to lean to turn. Second, and more importantly, my pride gets me in a lot of trouble. That day, pride almost literally came before the fall!

Ninety-nine percent of my sin can be traced to pride. Go ahead, fact-check it. When I'm selfish, unforgiving, judgmental, untruthful, arrogant, or self-loathing, it can all be traced to one thing: I think I'm the center of my world.

I'm also really good at playing down the danger of my pride. I mean, it's not as bad as (enter harmful-sounding sin), right? But unchecked, pride can have huge consequences, especially in how it affects our relationship with God. For example,

- if we think we know it all, we won't follow the Shepherd.
- if we can't admit when we're wrong, the Holy Spirit can't help us grow.
- if we believe we're better than others, we set ourselves up for judgment.
- if we think we can do it all, we'll chase perfection instead of accepting God's grace.
- if we're all about me, me, me, we'll miss opportunities to be Jesus's hands and feet to others.
- if we undervalue our worth (an ironic form of pride), we undermine God's creative genius in making us.

I have a feeling learning humility will be a lifelong lesson. Less of me, more of God's glory. Less of me, more of others' interests and well-being. I might not be the picture of humility yet, but at least I can now say I know how to drive a scooter (hashtag humblebrag).

Time to Shine

How could pride (i.e., thinking too highly of yourself, thinking about yourself too much, thinking you know better than God, etc.) affect each of these categories in your life? Put a star next to any you especially want to work on this week.

God: _____

_____

Relationships: _____

_____

Self-worth: _____

_____

Money: _____

_____

Body image: _____

_____

Future plans: _____

_____

Tip #40

When you know someone, you talk to them.

Lily has a great dad. When she was a little girl, she learned that her dad was kind because he looked after her, spoke kindly to her, and made sure she had everything she needed.

As Lily grew up, her dad was always there for her, offering advice and telling her she had what it took to change the world. When she made dumb choices, he gave her way more grace than she deserved. He told her he would never, ever stop loving her. And he meant that quite literally.

Not only does Lily know her dad is amazing because of the way he treats her and others, but he's told her about stuff he did before she was born that proves his character. She knows a lot about him. He's patient, honorable, a true romantic, and has a funny sense of humor. And she loves him for it.

Her dad talks to her all the time, but the crazy thing is, Lily never actually talks to him back. Even if he's right in front of her. She talks *about* him a lot: "My dad said . . . " or "I really like how my dad . . ." When he gives her an amazing gift (which happens often, because he loves to see her smile), she tells all her friends, "Look at this present my dad got me!" And he knows she's grateful. He just wishes she would tell *him* thank you.

It's probably the most awkward when it's just the two of them. They could be sitting right next to each other in the car, and Lily would still talk *about* her dad. She might glance over at him and say, "I really appreciate how my dad is always there for me." And he would smile, knowing she meant it, but a little sad too, because he knows their relationship would be so much stronger if she would just talk to him. After all, relationships rely on two-way communication.

I bet Lily's story sounded a bit farfetched, right? Who would actually do that? When you know someone, talking to them comes naturally.

Do me a favor. Read the first five paragraphs again, but this time, every time you see the words *her dad*, replace them with *God*.

Hit a little close to home? Yeah, me too. I know a lot about God, I'm really grateful for everything He's done for me, but if I'm not careful, I can go long stretches without talking straight to Him. I can act like He's not even there. How awkward.

One of the benefits of having a relationship with God is the privilege of talking to Him. He's the kind of dad who can appreciate the serious *and* the funny stuff, is always there to listen, and wants to hear it all. So, let's take advantage of two-way conversation that matches all we know about Him.

Time to Shine

Another name for talking to God is prayer. You can pray silently, out loud, or even write down your words. To help me stay in the habit of talking to God throughout the day, I've created some prayer routines. For example, I talk to God about the coming day right when I wake up and pray for my family when I get into the car in the morning. Whenever I fly, I write a letter to God in my journal. And as soon as I tell someone I'll pray for them, I set a reminder on my phone so I don't forget.

How about you? Write down three prayer habits you already have or could start this week to remind you to talk to God:

1. _____
   _____

2. _____
   _____

3. _____
   _____

Tip #41

You can't hear whispers at a concert. Make some quiet.

At six a.m., Lanie's alarm blares to life with a rousing chorus of Early Riser. Rubbing the sleep from her eyes, she pops in her earbuds to listen to her favorite "Feeling Happy" playlist while she gets ready. At breakfast, the blender whirs while she throws some lunch items into a paper sack. On the school bus, unruly students shout and tease each other, making it hard to concentrate on the English assignment she's trying to finish before first period.

At school, teachers lecture, announcements blare, bells ring. Volleyball practice comes next, with shouts of "mine" and "nice shot" echoing off the gym walls. On the car ride home, an ambulance's siren interrupts her and her dad's conversation. After two hours of homework, mixed with texting friends, she finally throws on her pajamas and rolls into bed. As she clicks off the light, Lanie slips into sleep, unaware that the sound of . . . *nothing* . . . is the first silence she's heard all day.

Maybe you can relate. It's a loud life, isn't it?

There's a story in the Bible about a time when the prophet Elijah needed to hear God's voice. A crazy queen had just vowed to kill him, so he was questioning his life choices while running far, far away. God wanted to remind him of some things Elijah couldn't hear in the chaos, so He told him to go up to a secluded mountain and wait in a cave. First Kings 19:11–13 tells us what happened next.

Then a great and powerful wind tore the mountains apart and shattered the rocks before the LORD, but the LORD was not in the wind. After the wind there was an earthquake, but the LORD was not in the earthquake. After the earthquake came a fire, but the LORD was not in the fire. And after the fire came a gentle whisper. When Elijah heard it, he pulled his cloak over his face and went out and stood at the mouth of the cave. Then a voice said to him, "What are you doing here, Elijah?"

God's Presence came in a whisper.

I don't know about you, but most days I'd need God to show up in the earthquake, fire, or wind in order for me to hear Him arrive. My life is loud—full of sounds, yes, but also distractions and busyness. Unless I actively make some quiet, I risk never hearing God's whispers. And that would be a shame, because I desperately want to hear what He has to say.

If you need to hear God tell you that He loves you, if you need His advice or perspective, it won't happen at a 24/7 concert of life. You'll probably have to turn off the music, set aside the phone, and pause the to-do list. Turn down the volume now and then. What you hear in the quiet will be worth it.

Time to Shine

When you're used to lots of noise, quiet can feel uncomfortable at first. It takes some practice to get used to sitting still, focusing, and listening. Take five minutes each day this week to just "be" with God. (Set a reminder if you think you'll forget.) Find a quiet spot free from distractions, take a few deep breaths, and invite God to join you. You may hear something specific from Him, you may not—there's no agenda. You're just creating quiet to talk to God and allow Him the opportunity to speak if He has something to say. Afterward, write down anything that stands out to you.

Tip #42

God's a good author. Trust His technique.

Fiction authors generally fall into one of two camps: the pantsers and the plotters. The pantsers—so named because they "fly by the seat of their pants"—find outlines a bore. Creativity must rein! Free from the constraints of a fixed plot, they set their characters loose in their imaginary world and tap their fingertips together like Gru, waiting to see what trials, mishaps, victories, or conflicts arise. If the author feels particularly happy and hopeful, you might see some rainbows and unicorns color the page. If their mood sours, a world might explode or a sidekick could self-combust. You just never know. And wherever those characters end up at the conclusion of 100,000 words, well, that's how the story was always meant to finish.

Plotters, on the other hand, have a plan for the plan. These authors have mapped out acts one through three, plus an epilogue, and entered key dates on a timeline app to make sure everything lines up just so. Their characters' fates are sealed, marching through predetermined obstacles and triumphs to the appointed finale. If a character starts to veer away from "The Plan," they're quickly shooed back into the outline. And at the end of 100,000 words, there are no surprises.

So, which method creates a better story, pantser or plotter? You'll find great authors in both camps, but in my experience, the best storytellers know how to weave both approaches together. They have a beginning and end in mind—along with maybe a handful of important landmarks along the way—but they also give their imagination space to explore the unexpected. They let the characters show a bit of attitude, make decisions they didn't see coming, and then adapt "The Plan" to fit new story developments.

They say fiction is a mirror of the world around us. And I've come to find that fiction—or in this case, writing it—teaches us a lot about God too.

The Bible describes Jesus as the author of our faith (see Hebrews 12:2). Which begs the question: Is God a pantser or a plotter?

Plotting is obviously part of His nature. Before God spoke any of His characters into existence, before He chose our setting, He already knew what the last page would hold (we'd be with Him forever!). He had a few key plot twists nailed down, like those He foretold through Old Testament prophets. But He's also a bit of a pantser, and I love Him for it. He's given His characters (us) free will, which means He's not controlling our every move. Sure, there are certain things He has clearly asked you to do (or not do), but He's also leaving room for you to make decisions of your own, based on your interests, circumstances, and personality. This blending of techniques not only makes God an incredible author, it makes this life one heck of a story.

Why does this matter? Well, how God approaches writing our stories not only tells us a lot about Him, it helps us know how to approach the decisions we'll have to make as the plot moves along.

Understanding God's approach takes a ton of pressure off when you have big choices to make. You don't have to panic about which college to go to, what job to take, or whether you'll be single or married someday. You don't have to worry that if you make the wrong choice, you'll leave "God's will" and ruin your life forever. As long as you're approaching the decision thoughtfully—asking God for guidance and inviting wise people who know you to share their perspective—you have the freedom to do what your faith inspires you to do.

On the flip side, understanding God's technique also keeps you from overplanning your future. (Shout out to the fellow "plan for the plan"-ers!) It's good to chart a course, but you can also trust God to write your story. Seriously—let Him do what He wants with it. Let Him take away things that might hurt you in the long run and allow Him to introduce pivot points that will deepen your character arc. (That's author talk for, "Your world might feel like it's falling apart, but you'll be stronger for it in the end.") Your story might not go how you expected, but you can trust that He has good things in store. He wants your brightest life for you too! After all, He's had your happy ending planned since page one.

Time to Shine

If Jesus is the author of your faith, your journey with God is its own great story. Obviously, it's not finished yet, but take some time to write out the story so far. How and when did it start? Have you met any trustworthy guides? What obstacles or doubts have you faced (or are facing now)? Why do you keep pressing on?

Tip #43

Don't drink poison and expect the other person to die. Forgive and live.

October 2, 2006, started like any other in the rural village of Nickel Mines, Pennsylvania. As an Amish community, the families prize simplicity over modern convenience for religious reasons. It wasn't unusual to see children arrive at the local one-room schoolhouse by horse and buggy, wearing traditional Amish clothing and hats.

That day, twenty-six children of various ages sat at wooden desks in the little schoolhouse, going about their studies as usual. But at 10:30 a.m., a thirty-two-year-old milk delivery driver from a nearby town entered the school. Forcing the boys and adults to leave, he barricaded the door and tied up the remaining eleven girls. When the police arrived outside, he began shooting. Charles Roberts killed five precious girls and wounded five others before taking his own life.

The tragedy rocked the world. It was unthinkable! How could anyone, let alone a father with children of his own, commit such a horrendous crime? People who had never heard of Nickel Mines wept in solidarity with the families who grieved. We were outraged.

But as details of the tragedy spread through every news channel in America, another story emerged that shocked us even further. The very families who had lost their girls—mourned daughters, sisters, cousins, and playmates—spoke of forgiveness. They offered condolences and genuine concern to the shooter's family. Some of them showed up to his funeral and formed a human wall to give the family privacy from news cameras. Someone else's sin had ripped out their hearts, and yet they said, "If we don't forgive, how can we be forgiven?"[1] (a reference to Matthew 6:14–15).

The path through grief for the families of Nickel Mines wasn't easy. They felt deep pain and unbelievable suffering. Yet in choosing to forgive, they saved themselves the further destruction of bitterness and revenge, two cancers that can eat a person until they're unrecognizable. That can drive a person to do something monstrous—like Charles Roberts did.

Unbeknownst to his family, Charles had been angry at God for a long time. He couldn't forgive Him for allowing his own daughter to die nine years earlier. He also couldn't forgive himself for something he had done in adolescence. That unforgiveness turned to bitterness, bitterness turned to anger, anger to hate, hate to revenge. In the end, his inability to forgive cost him—and others—everything.

You could say refusing to forgive is like drinking poison and expecting the other person to die.

Because of free will, there's a 100 percent chance you're going to be hurt by someone else's choices at some point in your life. By sins like violence, lies, betrayal, indifference, and anger. When that happens, you too will have a choice to make: forgive and move forward, or hold on to resentment until it destroys you.

Just so we're clear, forgiveness doesn't mean forgetting. It doesn't mean there aren't consequences for the person's actions. It simply means you give up your right to hold the sin against them

---

1. Terri Roberts, "My Son Shot 10 Amish Girls in a Pennsylvania Schoolhouse." *Women's Day*, published February 19, 2016. https://www.womansday.com/life/inspirational-stories/a53626/terri-roberts-forgiven-excerpt/. Article adapted from *Forgiven* by Terri Roberts with Jeanette Windle (Bethany House Publishers, 2015).

and trust God as judge. You let go, so what they did can't keep a grip on you. Like the Amish of Nickel Mines showed us, when you forgive, new life can grow from the ashes of your pain.

Time to Shine

As you read about forgiveness, did someone specific come to mind? Are you holding on to resentment that could keep you from living your best, brightest life? If so, take some time to process the hurt, then read Matthew 18:21–35. In light of all God has forgiven you for, ask Him to show you how to forgive too.

Tip #44

Break the silence about your secret sins. Freedom is worth it.

When I first launched LifeLoveandGod.com, one of my favorite features was the "Ask Jessie" page. Girls visiting the site could ask questions about anything in the world, and for a long time I was able to respond to each one personally. Obviously, I got lots of questions about boys, and plenty about body image and family dynamics too. Then, since questions could be asked anonymously, girls began finding courage to ask about the stuff *really* weighing on their hearts. Sexual addiction. Self-harm. Disordered eating. Substance abuse.

Many of these questions were from churchgoing, God-loving girls who felt completely powerless to stop doing what they didn't want to do. They were drowning, convinced that if they told anyone else about their secret sins, they'd be viewed as disgusting, faithless failures. And worst of all, they doubted God could forgive them because they kept *returning* to the same sin, over and over, even though they "knew better."

My heart broke. These beautiful girls had suffered so long in silence, questioning not just their choices but their worth. They clung to the lie that surviving meant hiding—appearing perfect at any cost. I felt their desperation as if I had walked in their shoes.

The truth was, I had.

Reading email after email, I knew it was time to break the silence about my own secrets. God had brought me too far not to.

As embarrassing as it would be, I needed to let other girls know they weren't alone.

When people hear I've written over a dozen books, they'll often ask which is my favorite. You could compare the question to inquiring which of my kids I'd save in an alien invasion. But one book does win the award, hands down, for being hardest to write: *Unashamed: Overcoming the Sins No Girl Wants to Talk About*. It's the book where I spilled the tea about a decade-plus sexual addiction on page one. (I figured it was best to jump in the deep end instead of inch in slowly.) It also wins a second award: most rewarding. I have a shoebox full of letters, printed emails, and notes from readers who finally realized that they weren't the only one—a truth maybe you need to hear too.

If you're trapped in a secret sin, no matter what it is, you're not alone. You can also never go too far, or be too far gone, for God's grace. God's enemy, Satan, would love to keep you isolated and drowning in shame. He wants to convince you you've got the issue under control, that you're better off keeping everything to yourself. Don't listen to a word of it. I know it might be hard to believe right now, but you can live free. With the Holy Spirit's help, you can accept God's forgiveness. You can change. It won't be easy—uncovering hurts, rewiring habits, and dying to self ain't a walk in the park. But take it from me, sister, freedom is worth any cost. It's time to break the silence and step into the light.

Time to Shine

While you read this chapter, did a secret struggle come to mind? Are you tired of letting it control you? If you need a first step or a big dose of hope, consider picking up a copy of *Unashamed: Overcoming the Sins No Girl Wants to Talk About.* I can't promise it will be everything you need, but it could be the first step you've been praying for. If you can't afford a copy, drop me a message at LifeLoveandGod. com and I'll send you one as my gift to help you on your journey. You'll also find a free resource hub for your fight against secret sins at LifeLoveandGod.com/unashamed.

Tip #45

You can't out-give God. But you should try.

God's generosity blows me away time and time again. It seems He gets a kick out of outdoing Himself. I could tell you dozens of stories—both mine and others'. Here's just one example from my life.

Paul and I had two young kids at home, and in that season we were living off of one income. That meant the bills were high and the bank accounts were low. During the girls' nap time, I began work on a book project that was strictly an act of faith. I had no promise that it would get published, but I felt God was daring me to write it. That's really the best way to describe it. It's like He had given me these pockets of time, along with a choice: use it to scroll social media or make it count by challenging and encouraging others with my words. I chose option two.

Eighteen months later, I still didn't know if it would ever be published. But I was so thankful to God for giving me the time and partnering with me to write those ten chapters, I told Him I'd give half of any money the book earned right back to Him.

A few months later, a prominent publisher bought the manuscript. (A miraculous story for another time.) They liked it so much that they offered to pay me *three times* the going rate for that type of book. We were able to make ends meet for another year, and with God's half, I had the joy of helping some awesome ministries—including building a home in Ethiopia for women in crisis.

Over and over again, when we give, He blesses more. That doesn't mean we give to get. It's not like we're throwing coins into a slot machine and pulling the lever because we want a bigger payout.

Religious formulas always backfire. But when we just choose to give with a genuine heart, Jesus makes good on His words, "Give, and it will be given to you" (Luke 6:38).

I've learned this principle applies to more than money. We also get blessed when we're generous with our time, our abilities, our energy, or even our words. I love the way Eugene Peterson paraphrases Luke 6:38 in *The Message:*

> Give away your life; you'll find life given back, but not merely given back—given back with bonus and blessing. Giving, not getting, is the way. Generosity begets generosity.

The more you give, the more you'll receive. So if you want to live a full-of-blessing kind of life, I dare you to try to out-give God.

Time to Shine

My father-in-law often says, "You've been blessed to be a blessing." What blessings has God given you that you can share with others instead of keeping them to yourself? Consider the categories below and write out ways you can give and who you'll give to.

Money: _____

Time: _____

Abilities: _____

Energy: _____

Kind or encouraging words: _____

Use the remainder of the page—or a journal—to record any unexpected return blessings.

Tip #46

Explore your doubts.
Don't stop there.

My friend Sean grew up in rural USA knowing about God from an early age. I'd be willing to bet he could sing all the VeggieTales songs, probably played a "wise man" in at least one Christmas pageant, and rarely missed Sunday school. In his teen years, his desire to understand God grew, and after high school he picked a private Christian college to attend. He could recite dozens of Bible verses, knew basic theology better than some pastors, and to everyone watching, he seemed like he was all in on this faith thing.

What none of us guessed was that Sean had growing doubts about God, His methods, and His people. He didn't dare ask questions though, because weren't good Christians supposed to know all the answers? So he prayed for more faith and tried harder to believe. Still, the doubts wouldn't leave. As the years passed, they ate at him, multiplying and simmering just under the surface. He got really good at pretending. By the time he graduated from college, leaving the "Christian bubble" for the first time in his twenty-two years, his doubts had grown so big he couldn't see past them. Instead of facing the questions head on and wrestling to find answers, he convinced himself God couldn't possibly exist and that everything he had believed was a sham. As far as I know, he still hasn't looked back.

I don't share that story to scare or shame you. I just have a hunch that, like Sean, maybe you've wrestled with some doubts of your own, like:

How could a good God let that happen?

If God's real, why doesn't He feel real?

If Adam and Eve were the only people, how could their son have married a woman from another town?

How could "God's people" act like such hypocrites?

If God is love, wouldn't He say all love is okay?

When was the earth actually created?

How can we be sure the Bible wasn't changed over time?

And those are just a few of mine! Yeah, I've been following God for decades now, and you know what? The longer I've lived, the more questions I've had. After careful searching, I've found answers to some; others might not get resolved until heaven, when I finally get to ask God for clarification.

I'm going to go out on a limb here and suggest that doubts are a natural part of following God with a sincere heart. When you truly want to know someone, you ask questions to figure out who they are. What makes them tick? Why do they do what they do? Personally, I think God welcomes our questions because it means we're trying to understand Him better. And it's not like He can't handle them!

Your church, friends, or even family might feel threatened by your questions, but God won't. Doubting isn't dangerous. Giving up on finding answers is.

God promises to be found if you seek Him with all your heart (Jeremiah 29:13). Looking for the truth takes time and effort.

Admitting where you were wrong takes humility. Accepting you might not get some answers in this life takes patience. Voicing your doubts takes courage, but working through them can lay the foundation for an unshakable faith and the relationship of a lifetime.

Time to Shine

Do you have questions or doubts about God, His ways, or His people? Write them down on a piece of paper.

Over the years, I've learned that some questions demand answers before others. You could think of them as levels of priority.

1. **ESSENTIAL BELIEFS** central to the Christian faith (like whether Jesus was a real person or if the Bible's trustworthy)

2. **CONVICTIONS** that are important, but genuine Christians still sometimes disagree on (like whether women can be pastors or how old the earth is)

3. **PREFERENCES** that really don't matter so much in light of eternity (like what type of worship music to play at church)

Using those categories as a guide, number each question you wrote down with a one, two, or three. Then commit to searching for answers, starting with the essentials.

Tip #47

You don't have to "feel" God to love Him.

My relationship with my husband, Paul, started out as attraction, watching his shenanigans at a Christian summer camp and playing volleyball together. It bubbled into chemistry during the years we sent literally hundreds of emails to each other. Seeing his name in my inbox brightened my mood like sunshine breaking through clouds.

Fast-forward a few years, and our first date had me as giddy as a kid going to Disneyland. The first time he took my hand, the feel of his skin touching mine sent electricity racing through my limbs. Looking into his eyes melted me completely. When we spent three months apart while I traveled overseas, I ached to have him by my side, like part of me was missing. When I heard him whisper "I love you" over the phone, my heart stood still. The longing was almost unbearable. On my return, when he asked me to spend forever with him, I don't know how I didn't float right up to the moon. Our first kiss felt like firecrackers; our honeymoon held the passion of a thousand happily ever afters.

I didn't have to work to feel strong emotions for my Paul—I couldn't seem to help myself. And all that attraction, chemistry, longing, and passion made me really confident in our relationship.

But *love* isn't a feeling. Love is a choice, a choice I have had to make daily in the years since, even when jobs, kids, frustrations, and disappointed dreams have sometimes stripped us numb. When the ordinary dulls emotion, love inspires me to continue getting to know Paul, to respect and care for him, to be patient and kind and committed. (Though let's be clear, not perfectly!) My feelings come and go, but love remains because I choose it each day.

There have been times when my relationship with God has been firecrackers and goose bumps too. Moments I've felt so seen and known that my heart could burst from longing to spend forever with Him. When His presence feels tangible—like I could reach out and take His hand—it's easy to feel confident in my relationship with Him. But love isn't a feeling. It's a choice, a choice I have had to make daily, even when busyness, doubts, distance, and disappointed dreams have stripped me numb.

If God feels distant, it doesn't necessarily mean something is wrong with you or your relationship. Even if you *never* feel God the way others describe experiencing Him, that doesn't mean you aren't His. You can still choose to get to know God, to respect and praise Him, to be holy and obedient and committed. He still wants—and receives—your love, even if you're not overcome with emotion during worship or brought to tears when you pray.

Just like in a romantic relationship, your feelings for God might come and go. If you find yourself in a dry season emotionally—for a short time or long stretch—focus on choosing love for Him each day. Because, unlike emotions, love can last a lifetime.

Time to Shine

You could think of God's presence like a beach bonfire. The closer you stand to the fire, the more you'll feel its warmth, see the beauty of the twisting flames, and notice its sparks rising into the night sky. The farther you stand from it, the colder you'll feel, the less you'll notice its beauty, and the harder it will be to roast gooey marshmallows. The fire is there either way. It's up to you whether to take advantage of it.

Write God a note to talk about your relationship. Be honest about how close or far you feel from Him and tell Him how you'd like your relationship to be in the future. What steps will you take to draw closer to His warmth?

Tips About Mindset

If your brain is like a supercomputer, you could think of mindset as the operating system. It runs in the background but affects how you approach everything. A resilient, positive, adaptable attitude will help you keep life bright.

Tip #48

Sometimes "childhood you" needs to be remembered.

Once upon a time, there was a little girl who wore a tutu over footie pajamas and laughed even when no one was looking. When she heard her favorite toddler songs, she sang loud and danced louder. After nap time, she played with her dolly and built towers out of blocks. At night, she lined her stuffed friends along the perimeter of her bed just so, and, after reading and prayer, shared special kisses with her mommy. She never tired of playing make-believe with her friends, and when given the smallest role, she just asked to play again. Again and again. The girl was loved. And the girl was happy.

Time did what time will do, and the little girl grew some. She outgrew her footie pajamas, traded her dolly for an American Girl with fancy outfits, and played Legos for hours. Sometimes, she sang along to her favorite songs and danced when no one was watching. When her family moved to a new town, she was quick to be kind, giving little gifts to her classmates. She never tired of inviting kids to play. Even when they stopped saying yes, she found the courage to ask again. Again and again. Yet the girl was loved. And the girl was happy.

Time did what time will do, and the little girl grew some more. She packed her doll and Legos into boxes and checked her outfit in the mirror before leaving for school. Each day she carried a backpack full of textbooks, but the weight of insecurity was heavier. She learned that kindness doesn't always make you the friends you want, and worried "he" would never notice her. When she heard her favorite songs, she was careful not to sing too loud. She never tired of checking her phone, and when she wasn't included, she tried harder to fit in again. Again and again. The girl wondered if she was loved. And the girl was rarely happy.

But time will do what time will do, and the little girl will grow some more. She'll pack her room into boxes and make her way into the great big world. When she moves to a new town, she'll make friends by being kind, and she'll see that she herself is a gift to others. At night, she'll wonder why she cared so much what everyone else thought about her, and make peace with the parts of her she wanted to change. She'll sing loud to every song, and when life pushes her down, she'll let God help her back up again. Again and again. Because the girl will know she is always loved. And I hope, once again, she'll be happy.

Time to Shine

- What were you like when you were younger?
- How are you still that way? How are you different?
- What parts of your younger self do you want to keep today? As you become an adult?

Tip #49

Have a vision for your life.

The first time I saw it, I cried. It wasn't that I hadn't tackled a hard-core renovation before. It's just that, on the heels of an especially painful move in the middle of a pandemic, I was fresh out of resolve. Like zero motivation, to be honest. So I just sat on the floor and stared blurry-eyed at my new kitchen—with missing cabinet doors, drooping ceiling, rotting floorboards, and scattered rodent turds.

After said good cry, I realized I had only two options: give up or dig in and do what I could to make the place home. The first option sounded highly tempting, not gonna lie. But Jesus had seen me through worse than this, so I figured I owed it to Him to give it a go.

If I was going to build enough momentum for a complete gut job, I knew I needed a plan. Inspiration. A crystal clear vision. So I started bookmarking inspo photos online and browsed home improvement stores. I evaluated what had worked (and flopped) in past houses, watched *Fixer Upper* reruns to channel my inner Joanna Gaines, and made a detailed budget.

Before I even started the demo, I could picture what the kitchen would look like when I was done: a bright little paradise where people would eat good food and tell stories around the island. That starry-eyed vision carried me through every high and low of the project. It gave me motivation to build eighteen cabinets and courage when a water leak flooded the new drywall a day after installation. It guided my decisions about countertops and cabinet pulls, helped determine when to splurge on a light fixture or save on a faucet. In all, the project took four months, sixteen borrowed tools, and two friends coming to the rescue. But now? Now my kitchen is just as I envisioned it could be, complete with stories and good food around the butcher block island.

Like a home renovation, having a vision for our lives can make or break the outcome. You'll move toward what you picture—what you can get excited about. If you have a vision, then the decisions you make today, tomorrow, and a year from now are going to get you closer to your goals.

For example, if you had a vision of studying abroad for a semester in college, it would help you decide whether you'd go to college at all, then which school you'd choose, and eventually which classes you'd take to qualify. Another example: If you see yourself married someday to a God-fearing guy, that's going to affect decisions you make today about relationships—like what kind of guy you're willing to date and the type of person you aim to become. Make sense?

Now a quick disclaimer: This isn't about naming and claiming the particulars of your future, and it's not a New Agey mindfulness trick to make all your dreams come true. Like, you might be able to picture with perfect clarity living happily ever after with Gavin Casalegno, but it's probably not going to happen. Last I checked, God was the one ultimately directing our steps (Proverbs 16:9). I'm talking about broad brushstrokes, casting a general vision that leaves room for Him to surprise you with a better, more fulfilling, or even more challenging route.

If you want to move intentionally toward your brightest life, start filling a mental vision board with "pictures" of your future. Who do you want to be and what do you want your life to look like when you graduate high school? What about your twenty-first birthday? Your twenty-fifth? What hobbies do you want to master? How do you picture your health? What kind of relationships do you hope to have? Do you see yourself enjoying a particular type of career? Do you want to be a stay-at-home parent? Do you want to travel the world or become a master welder?

You might find the actual details of your future life look a bit different than what you picture now, but with God's guidance and some good decision-making on your part, I have no doubt you'll find it even more fulfilling than you envision.

Time to Shine

Start a "My Life" vision board where you can pin photos, destinations, programs, and lifestyles that excite you. It could be a physical poster in your room, a folder in a notebook, or even a social media account, as long as it's a place you can visualize where you want to go in life. Ask God for inspiration that both highlights your personality and honors Him.

Tip #50

You have a choice. It's kind of a superpower.

During the college semester I spent in Israel, the professors gave us a week-long "study break." That sounded like code for "more traveling" to me, so a few friends and I hopped an all-night train to Egypt with thin wallets and stuffed Jansports.

The five of us spent the next six days riding camels around the pyramids in Cairo, exploring an ancient temple in Luxor, hiking from the Valley of the Kings to the temple of Hatshepsut, and accidentally purchasing fake train tickets. I can still smell the jasmine and lotus flower "essences" peddled at perfume shops, taste the savory koshari from street vendors, and feel the heat of the desert sun at noon. But when I think about my time in Egypt, one encounter impacted me most: meeting Ali Blue Eyes.

We ran into Ali along the banks of the Nile River in Luxor. He had a boat, and offered us an hour-long sail for only fifteen Egyptian pounds (about $4.50). A deal even broke college kids could afford. We gratefully boarded his small felucca, the *Mary Rose*, and found seats along the wooden deck. We sailed down the river, taking in velvet fields of grasses dotted with palm trees made all golden in early-evening sun, water lapping softly against the hull. But even with the amazing view, as we sailed, I still found myself drawn to our captain. It was obvious how he got his name—his eyes were *bright* blue, a stark contrast to the majority of Egyptians we had met.

Ali Blue Eyes spoke decent English, and since he seemed about our age, we made small talk while he sailed. I asked him if he was in college too. I've never forgotten his response.

Ali wanted to go to school. Very much. But his father had skipped out, and as the oldest son, he was responsible to provide for his mother and siblings. So he worked every day in the hope he could save enough to do both. What struck me most about his explanation was not how sad it was, though it felt unfair that he carried so much weight for someone so young. It wasn't even embarrassment, though I was ashamed I took my education for granted so often, let alone the chance to travel. No, what has remained with me all these years was the determination in Ali's arresting eyes. Despite his "disadvantaged" circumstances, Ali believed he had choices, and he was going to make the most of them.

Some circumstances are out of our control. Ali couldn't change the fact his dad left, but he still had decisions to make. He could have bailed on his family too, but instead he tried to provide for and do right by them. He chose to get up early every day to hustle shuttling tourists up and down the Nile. He chose to save his extra money for an education someday instead of blowing it on drinks with his buddies after work. And maybe most powerful of all, he chose to hope. That's what I saw in his eyes.

The power of choice is one of the greatest gifts God has given you. It's honestly kind of a superpower. The vast majority of circumstances, accomplishments, habits, and your future will be affected—even determined—by the choices you make. If you make stupid choices with your gift, you'll have fewer options to choose from. But if you make mindful decisions, your choices have unparalleled power to set you up for a life you'll love.

Time to Shine

Let's practice thinking through the logical effects of your choices. Consider how the following might steer your life, then add a few more to each list.

SIMPLE DAILY CHOICES THAT HAVE LIFE-SHAPING EFFECTS

- Brushing your teeth
- Saving more than you spend
- Doing your homework
- Letting someone else go first
- Telling the truth
- Skipping junk food
- _____
- _____
- _____

BIGGER CHOICES THAT HAVE LIFE-STEERING EFFECTS

- When you'll start dating
- Whether you'll get married
- Where (or whether) you'll attend college
- What defines success for you
- Where you'll live
- Whether you'll have children
- _____
- _____
- _____

Tip #51

Feed what you want to grow.

When I was eleven, my best friend and I decided to create our own line of skin care products. More specifically, we wanted to make a signature face mask that would wow our family and friends into shelling out hard cash. Our entrepreneurial vision was seeing dollar signs. We decided to use "all-natural," "local-sourced" ingredients. Read: We were broke and would have to forage in my fridge and backyard for our supplies. What can I say? We were eco-chic before it was of the moment.

We got to work on our recipe. Something creamy for the base. Mayonnaise? Sure, why not. Egg white for some shine? Brilliant. A snip of Mom's aloe plant? We could already picture our own glowing skin practically selling product for us.

But something was still missing. Something exotic that would really set our mask above the competition. In a flash of genius, it came to me. I knew just the thing. Running outside, I "harvested" some of the stringy algae growing in a drainage channel on my street and proudly returned to the kitchen. My best friend agreed: our secret ingredient would make business explode.

We blended everything together until smooth, poured the bright green mixture into a large glass jar, and placed it on the top shelf of the fridge. We'd figure out our business model the next time she came over.

"Next time" kept getting pushed. A week passed, then two. We got distracted with school and life. I all but forgot about our mask-making business until the morning I heard my mom scream, "Jessica Ann!"

Apparently, our secret ingredient—the unspecified algae I had scraped off the road—really had made *something* explode, namely the glass jar. The fridge was covered in green slime, glass shards everywhere. See, I failed to realize that mixing blended algae with those other ingredients just gave a million tiny algae a lifetime supply of food. They grew and grew—eventually becoming unstoppable—because I fed them. Without even knowing it.

What you feed will grow too. That's true of homemade face masks and it's just as true of a million other things in life.

Let's get real. If I have a lust issue, reading steamy novels is only going to feed my sin. If I struggle with self-hate, watching videos of "perfect" influencers will feed those insecurities. Selfishness loves to be fed attention. Laziness, distraction.

On the flip side, if I want to feed my faith, I could feast on my Bible or go to a Christian summer camp. If I want to grow more hope, I might binge on positive music. Confidence will grow when I take risks and feed my soul grace instead of being so hard on myself. Focus feeds on balance. Kindness, love.

Yeah, it sounds simplistic, I know. But this principle has a lot of power in your life. The key is taking time to notice what you want to grow more of, and on the flip side, to identify what's growing that might get out of control someday. Feed intentionally, and you'll grow exponentially.

Time to Shine

- List three qualities or thoughts that you want to grow so they become bigger in your life.
- Give at least one specific way you plan to feed each of those this week.
- What do you need to stop feeding before it gets out of control?

Tip #52

Women are women. But your version of womanhood can be unique.

Picture the stereotypical 1950s housewife, and you'll have a pretty good image of Jane. She irons the laundry in perfect hair and makeup, cooks dinner each night with practiced ease, and keeps her prized rosebushes trimmed just so. Even after her kids grew up, she stayed home to keep house and support her husband, and she still does, sixty years after saying "I do." But talk to her for five minutes and you'll walk away more in love with Jesus. Her bookshelves are lined with dozens of completed Bible studies, evidence of her passion for God's Word and teaching other women about Him.

Lexi couldn't appear more different. She wears her hair cropped under a trucker hat, usually black, which matches half-inch lobe plugs and forearm tattoos. She doesn't have kids, and I'd be surprised if she owns an iron. But talk to her for five minutes and you'll also walk away more in love with Jesus. When she leads worship, her beautiful voice and heartfelt posture make room for the Spirit to move.

I've learned a lot from both Jane and Lexi about what womanhood looks like. Because true womanhood isn't defined by culture—it's defined by God. And He has a love for variety, remember?

There's freedom when we separate being female, which we are, from a particular culture's made-up ideas about what a woman *should* do, how she *should* act, and where her interests *should* lie.

I hate those "shoulds." I cringe when we paste absolutes on something God hasn't. The Bible's list of nonnegotiable, solely female characteristics is *really* short. More often, God calls both men *and* women to the same ideals: ditch pride, love Him, serve others. Then He gives us freedom to explore what that looks like for us as male or female, in our particular time in history, in our culture.

Yes, our bodies, our thought processes, even our emotional ranges are different. Men generally tend toward certain skills, strengths, and interests, and women to others. (By the way, we combine these differences to reflect the full image of God, which is really cool!) But those are generalities rather than rules. If a guy wants to be a stay-at-home dad, or if you want to rebuild engines, good on you. If you love to cook and keep house, embrace it and don't let anyone look down on you for it. A woman is a woman, whether she wants a collection of kids, power tools, or a combination of both.

Satan would love for you to question whether you're "really" a girl, or to wish you were a guy because they have it "easier." Why? Because those lies could easily sidetrack you from stepping into the unique, purpose-filled woman God designed you to be. A woman ready to change the world!

If Jesus were to paraphrase Matthew 20:25–28 in light of cultural gender norms, I imagine He might say something like:

"Look, the outside world is all about who's better: men or women. But in my kingdom, that's not even an issue! Your greatness isn't defined by your sex, it's defined by how willing you are to serve others. So quit worrying about others' view of your abilities, roles, and weaknesses, and start focusing on giving your life for others— just like I did."

Whoa. I'll take a side of conviction with that, please and thank you!

Your version of womanhood will be a unique reflection of you—your abilities, strengths, and interests. Instead of worrying about what a girl "should" do, allow the Holy Spirit to make you more like Jesus, so you can ditch pride, love God, and serve others with all of your XX chromosomes.

Time to Shine

Circle the following characteristics and interests that describe you. Don't worry about whether you "should" circle them. Add any others that come to mind. Then thank God for the unique version of womanhood you represent.

Artistic

Love kids

Like to build things

Talkative

Athletic

Nurturing

Focused

Strong

Like to shop

Okay with getting dirty

Empathetic

Less emotional

Enjoy makeup

Driven

Problem-solver

Tip #53

You don't have to possess it to enjoy it.

I'm a bit of a plant nerd. Okay, a lot of one. There's just something about the smell of fresh-turned, rich earth; the vivid green of itty-bitty seedlings in spring; the juicy perfection of a sweet strawberry just plucked from the stem. I don't know, maybe I'm part wood nymph. Plants just make me irrationally happy.

I've had a hidden Pinterest board of epic gardens for years— the kind with rustic wood arbors and climbing grapevines, raised beds full of flowers and at least a dozen different kitchen herbs. My real-life gardens have mostly consisted of mismatched containers in our various backyards, because it's hard to create an epic garden when your space is tiny or you live a mile high in a snowy climate. So when I moved to one of the best agricultural areas in California, renting a small house with a big dirt yard, I signed up for plant catalogs before the boxes were unpacked.

My landlords were gracious enough to support my idea of a garden. I staked out the corners and measured how much fencing I would need. I borrowed books on garden design and bookmarked my favorite raised beds online. The deck became a holding place for the fruit trees I couldn't wait to plant. I could almost taste the avocados and mandarins I'd be picking in no time.

Just as I began digging holes for the corner posts, a problem with the property's well cut the plans of my dream garden short. There wasn't enough water to support the houses *and* irrigate six hundred square feet of plants. That meant no garden for Jessie.

I'd be lying if I said I wasn't disappointed. Crushed would be more accurate. But a few weeks later, a kind neighbor approached me with an offer. Debbie had a beautiful garden, but not as much time as she needed to care for it. Would I be interested in sharing her garden with her? The offer was more than generous, and I gratefully accepted. I was soon in heaven working in Debbie's garden, surrounded by mature avocado and pomegranate trees, raised beds full of baby sprouts, and a proper strawberry patch. She generously shared her space and the harvests; I got my fill of fresh-turned dirt *and* made a new friend.

One day, as I was weeding between rows of arugula and garlic, it hit me that sharing a garden was yet another example of a lesson God has been trying to teach me my entire life. I don't have to *possess* something in order to enjoy it. In other words, it's possible to appreciate and benefit from something beautiful, cool, inspiring, or majestic even if I have no claim of ownership over it. My selfish nature wants every good thing exclusively for myself. In response, God often says, "Yes, that's a good thing, but it's not my best for you."

A dream garden is just one of a long list of things I've had to learn to *enjoy* without making them *mine*. I wouldn't have minded owning my friend Abby's gorgeous red Mustang, but I still got to ride shotgun and feel the wind in my hair after our rock climbing sessions. I wanted to call Toby mine, but in the absence of a romantic relationship, I could still enjoy his friendship and the way he brought so much fun and laughter to our friend group. I wanted to possess "perfect" beauty like my friend Sarah's, but I could still find joy in acknowledging God's handiwork in hers. I'd love to own an ocean-view house, but I can enjoy the sunset just as well walking on the public beach.

The happiest people I've met don't own everything they want; they make the most of what they have. If you can learn to appreciate the beautiful, luxurious, handsome, and inspiring things and people in life without having to "own" them, then you'll likely find you already possess everything you really need. It's a lesson I'm still learning as I trim, weed, and water in Debbie's garden.

Time to Shine

Let's get practical. List three things you'd really like to be yours but God has said no to (at least for now). It might be a relationship, nice stuff, a certain place, or whatever else comes to mind. Try to be specific. Then, next to each one, write down one or two ways you can enjoy or benefit from that thing, even if you never possess it for yourself.

1. _____

2. _____

3. _____

Tip #54

You do some pretty strange things. Question why.

In eighth grade, I had a computer teacher we'll call Mrs. M. Mrs. M was an energetic middle-aged woman, with thick, curly hair and a slight Israeli accent. She put up with zero shenanigans, but we liked her because she sometimes let us stay in at lunch to play computer games while trading food items with our friends. It was hard to earn our class's respect, but she managed to.

That's why I was so conflicted the day she wore a sleeveless dress to class. See, Mrs. M didn't shave her armpits, and judging by my classmates' reactions, you'd think she had grown a third arm. The boys knew to keep the snickers and snide comments quiet enough to avoid detention, but I'd be surprised if she didn't hear them anyway.

Since no one was brave enough to mention the social faux pas to Mrs. M directly, they turned their questions to her son, who unfortunately for him, happened to be in our class.

"Why doesn't your mom shave her pits, man? That's so weird!"

I can still picture his cheeks glowing red with embarrassment as he tried to change the subject.

To be honest, at the time, I was a little weirded out by it too. I mean, weren't women *supposed to* shave under their arms? Wasn't it unsanitary or something not to? We shaved our legs as well, especially as a nosy sixth grader might say something mean like, "Why are your legs so hairy?" to you on the bus, and then you'd have to sneak your mom's white disposable razor to make sure you fit in with the other girls . . . not that I knew from personal experience or anything. These were just things girls did. Right?

Turns out, I was wrong. It wasn't so long ago that shaving off perfectly good hair was considered a strange fad, not the other way around.

In the early 1900s, an American razor manufacturer named King C. Gillette realized he could double his sales if he could double the people who needed razors. He already had men's business, but if he could convince women they could benefit from a shave, voilà! He'd be a rich(er) man. Thus began a very clever marketing campaign convincing American women that smooth pits were less offensive and classier than au naturel.

Meanwhile, as women's hemlines shortened, girls started wearing nylons to make sure their legs were still modestly covered. During World War II, however, the government commandeered all that nylon for parachutes and such, which led to a big pantyhose shortage. So women started shaving the hair from their legs and painting them with skin-colored "leg paint" to make it look like they were still wearing nylons. Leg paint then got rationed too, but the shaving trend continued well after the war—and within a couple of decades, we had a new normal in women's fashion. Though when you think about it, it is kind of weird that we spend so much time and money getting rid of something as harmless as a little hair.

Look, whether you want to shave your legs, pits, arms, or anywhere else is completely up to you. You'll get no judgment from me! All I'm suggesting is that you ask yourself *why* you do the things you do, and make sure the answer isn't *only* "because everyone else is doing it."

Unless something goes against God's clear instructions or your parents' rules, you have freedom to follow cultural norms or buck them off. Sometimes it'll be worth following the crowd to avoid offending someone; other times following your heart will keep you safe or show the world an important point of view. From beauty practices to stuff you do online, from what you eat or drink to your educational path, be curious. Take a look at your actions. Question your motives. Then be brave enough to do you, regardless of whether ignorant people snicker.

Time to Shine

Get curious about the "why" behind the things you do today. Jot down anything that seems a bit odd now that you think about it. When you have time, do a little self-reflection and/or research. For each thing you write down, ask:

1. When did I start doing this?

2. Why did I start doing it?

3. Why do I do it now?

4. Do I want to (or should I) keep doing it?

Tip #55

Tame your thoughts and your emotions will follow.

One time in college, my friend Sarah asked if I'd be willing to cover a babysitting job for her so she could spend time with her boyfriend. I didn't have plans and needed the cash, so it was an easy yes. When I arrived, I met the dad, who introduced me to their six-year-old son, gave some instructions about dinner and bedtime, and showed me around the house—the normal routine. When his wife emerged from the bathroom looking lovely and smelling of fancy perfume, they kissed their son goodbye and headed out on their special date. *I've got this*, I thought.

Now, I was no Mary Poppins, but I had done a bit of childcare in my twenty-odd years of life, so I kind of knew the drill: mac 'n' cheese, coloring, board books at bedtime, and such. He ate his dinner without a fuss and even said he wanted to go to bed early so we'd have more time to read. What babysitter would turn down an offer like that? *This is the best job ever,* I thought.

What came next, though, turned the "best job" into a mental fright-fest.

It started when the house phone rang. Not wanting the loud *brriiiing* to wake the child who had finally fallen asleep, I picked it up quickly.

"Hello, this is the so-and-so's residence," I said.

Rhythmic breathing pulsed in the receiver.

"Hello?"

Click.

My palms instantly turned sweaty. I grabbed a copy of *Golf*

Digest from the coffee table and tried to distract myself. Five minutes later, the phone rang again. My stomach did somersaults, but I picked it up.

This time, a man's voice rasped, "I can see you."

My heart pounded through my chest. I forced myself to check the row of floor-to-ceiling living room windows. I couldn't see anything in the dark night.

"Who is this?" I managed.

"Someone who knows you're alone. I can see your blond hair through the window."

I froze. "This isn't funny. Who—"

Click.

I'm actually going to die, I thought.

I spent the next sixty seconds frozen in limb-melting fear, wondering if I should run, look for a weapon, or hide the small child I was now responsible for. Thinking about the options made me feel worse.

What felt like an eternity later (even though it was barely a minute), the phone rang again. Don't ask me why I picked it up. I guess the only thing worse than facing a potential axe murderer would be waking a sleeping child? Lifting the receiver with trembling fingers, I pressed it to my ear, but didn't say anything.

"Jess?" This time it was a girl's voice. "Jess, it's Sarah . . ."

My friend sounded irritated but gentle. She explained that when she told her boyfriend I was filling in for her, he thought it would be funny to scare the jujubes out of me.

I'm actually going to kill him, I thought.

Let me start by saying that if you ever suspect you're about to get murdered, dialing the police is a logical and reasonable approach. (Not sure why that didn't occur to me at the time.) Now that I know the whole thing was just a lame joke, I can laugh—and learn a thing or two. Top lesson: it's possible to feel *big* feelings that are based on completely false facts.

The objective truth is that I was no more or less safe while tucking in Junior than I was while gripping the phone in a dark living room. Why did I go from feeling relaxed and happy about an "easy" babysitting job to sweaty-palmed, heart-racing, fight-or-flight fear? Because my emotions followed my thoughts. When I thought, *All is well with the world*, I felt safe. When I thought, *I'm starring in a real-life horror flick*, I felt fear, whether it was true or not.

Philippians 4:8–9 (NLT) says,

> Fix your thoughts on what is true, and honorable, and right, and pure, and lovely, and admirable. Think about things that are excellent and worthy of praise.... Then the God of peace will be with you.

Notice that the feeling (peace) comes after the thinking (true, right, lovely thoughts). That's because your thoughts create your emotions. Control your thoughts, then, and you'll (largely) control how you feel.

My babysitting story is a funny example, but this truth affects so many critical areas of life. You aren't destined to feel helpless, sad, or anxious forever. You have a say in who you like. You can choose joy, even when circumstances stink. How?

1. Notice the negative emotion.

2. Identify the underlying thought.

3. Replace the thought with a better one (something that's true *and* positive).

I can't promise you'll never have unwanted or negative emotions, but if you practice those steps, you'll be a much happier, more peace-filled person. And as a side perk, if a friend's crazy boyfriend ever prank calls you while you're babysitting, you won't let fear stop you from calling 911. (Though, hopefully he'll come clean before law enforcement shows up!)

Time to Shine

Let's practice taming our thoughts. I've given some common but unhelpful thoughts on the left and the resulting emotions. On the right, jot down a better thought to replace them and the emotions you think might result. I've done the first couple to get you thinking.

THOUGHT	EMOTION	NEW THOUGHT	NEW EMOTION
I don't *want to* like him (or her). I just can't help it.	Desire	I admire that person, but they aren't best for me.	Content-ment
My mom is so annoying.	Irritation	It's nice to have someone who cares enough to look out for me.	Gratitude
My life sucks and will never be any better.	Despair		
I'm so ugly.	Self-hate		
I have to lie or I'll get in trouble.	Fear		

Tip #56

Like a good sauce, gratitude makes anything taste better.

Last week, I made the best sauce I've ever tasted in my life. The creamy, tangy mix of avocado, lime, garlic, and cilantro was partying in my mouth like New Year's Eve circa 1999. You know me and that I never exaggerate (*ever*), but this sauce could have been the best the world has ever seen or will see henceforth. Never mind that all I did was follow the recipe; I've still asked Food Network when they'd like a pilot of my new show: *Kick Booty Sauces with Jessie*.

My culinary skills may not qualify me for the next *Top Chef*, but I do know that a great sauce can turn flavorless chicken into BBQ bliss, plain pasta into Grandma's famous spaghetti, or a fish stick in a tortilla into a Baja-worthy fish taco. A little secret sauce can transform ordinary fare into food worth savoring.

I'd argue that thankfulness stars as the secret sauce of life. It can turn a bland existence into an extraordinary adventure. Gratitude has the ability to literally transform the way we see the world, and then make us people that others savor too.

I didn't always feel that way. Some time ago, a book deal I had been working on for a while fell through, cancer took my mom, I was floundering at parenting, and I was also struggling to figure out the "new normal" with my husband. My circumstances felt like I had dropped a pot of tomato sauce onto the kitchen floor . . . and then that happened too. Yeah, gratitude wasn't the first thing on my mind.

One day a friend gave me a book called *One Thousand Gifts* by Ann Voskamp. In it, she shares her journey of writing down things she was thankful for each day, and how that simple practice transformed her life. She said, "As long as thanks is possible, then joy is always possible."[1] And it turned out she was right. As I started my own log of the few things I felt grateful for, the list began multiplying, as did new, unexpected joy.

Thankfulness doesn't change the shape of your circumstances, but it does shape your outlook.

The crazy thing is, you always, always, *always* have something to be thankful for. Even in the hardest moments of life. Even when your boyfriend breaks up with you in a text. Even when your ACL snaps right before the biggest game of your life. Even when your dad loses his job, your church splits, or you don't make the cast. Even when your friend ghosts you, or your hair will *not* stinking cooperate. We can thank God in everything—even when we have to dig down deep to find a reason—because thankfulness doesn't depend on our situation. Like a good sauce, thankfulness actually *flavors* our circumstances.

Grateful people tend to be happier people. Maybe that's why God reminds us over and over in the Bible to be thankful, even in the hardest places and spaces. If you want a bright life, look on the bright side! Be the kind of girl who makes the best of a bad situation, and season your circumstances with the tangy goodness of gratitude.

---

1. Ann Voskamp. *One Thousand Gifts: A Dare to Live Fully Right Where You Are* (Zondervan, 2011), p. 33.

Time to Shine

Start your own "Bright Side List." You could include people, opportunities, small treasures, or big surprises you're thankful for. Keep writing them down day by day until you reach one hundred gifts from God. At the end, write a few sentences reflecting on how the project changed your perspective and your emotions.

Tip #57

Easy is easy. Work at things that last.

Baldassare Forestiere—let's call him Baldy for short—was twenty-two and longed to pursue his dream of becoming a citrus farmer. So in 1901, he left his hometown of Filari, Sicily, and made the long journey to wild and wonderful California. But when he got to Fresno, he realized two things. First, below the top two feet of soil, the ground turned to duripan, which is fancy talk for cement-like dirt that's almost impossible to dig through. Second, the summers were wicked hot.

Instead of giving up, though, Baldy got to thinking. He had grown up seeing beautiful Roman and Greek architecture in Europe. What if he could create something significant out of this rich but rock-hard dirt? Armed with nothing but a pick ax, a shovel, a wheelbarrow, and a sharp mind, he got to work. For the next forty years, he dug and he dug, fashioning stone blocks from the duripan, which he used to create sixty-five underground rooms, courtyards, passageways, and gardens. That's right, *underground gardens,* up to twenty feet below the surface, with skylights and a watering system. He grew his beloved oranges, grapefruits, and lemons, plus a bunch of other unique fruits. Some of the trees are still there today, now over a hundred years old.

His underground house solved both problems: He was able to use the very duripan that made farming difficult. And the cave-like rooms were up to twenty degrees cooler in the summer. Win-win.

When Baldy moved to Fresno with his big dream, he could

have taken the easy route. He could have bought a little stick-built house like everyone else and hammered away at the duripan to plant traditional orchards . . . and today the house and trees would be long gone. But because he chose to dig deeper, work harder, and think outside the norm, he created something awesome with lasting value.

Chances are slim that your lifelong dream includes citrus farming or digging an underground house. Mine neither. But after visiting Baldy's masterpiece—walking through those cool passageways, marveling at ancient grapevines twisting up through skylights in the ground—I've been thinking about ways you and I can skip easy in favor of lifelong impact. We could . . .

- read a whole book instead of bits and pieces of posts.
- make a home-cooked meal instead of grabbing fast food.
- start a business instead of killing time during summer break.
- end the dysfunctional relationship instead of staying just 'cause he's the safe bet.
- talk to the annoying new kid instead of ignoring him.
- take the job with the nonprofit instead of the high-paying one that will be miserable.
- start the book you've been dreaming of writing.
- (if you find the right guy) choose marriage instead of avoiding commitment.

When I think about the things I've done so far that have made the most impact, every single one of them took monumental effort. Easy has its place. But if you want to go further in life, work hard at things that will last.

Time to Shine

- What are some of your greatest accomplishments? What did it take to achieve them?
- Do you have a dream that sounds amazing but would take a lot of work?
- How could working hard at things that last apply to people and relationships?

Tip #58

Critique will melt a fragile ego, but inspire a resilient girl to do better.

The day I started writing my first novel, I sat frozen, staring at a blank computer screen. It felt like someone had dumped a mountain-sized pile of bricks in front of me and said, "Here, build a house." I had no idea if I could do it, let alone where the windows and doors were supposed to go. But since God had inspired me to give it a go, I was determined to see it through, no matter how long it took. That last bit turned out to be handy, because it took me over a year just to finish the first draft. When I held those warm pages in my hand, fresh off my printer, I could have floated to the moon. *I did it! I actually wrote a whole novel!* I couldn't wait to see what my group of test readers thought.

Within a few weeks, I started to get their feedback. Most of the readers thought it was pretty good, and they had polite suggestions for spicing up the plot or adjusting the wording—nothing too major. What a relief! After putting in so much work, I was ready to make those tweaks and call it good.

Then I got feedback from the last reader. Let me summarize: the writing itself—the *entire* 100,000-word manuscript—needed to be "elevated." She included dozens of pages with her suggestions marked so I could see what she meant. If you've ever gotten an essay back from a teacher half-covered with red pen, then you understand the gut punch I felt. Just multiply the humiliation by three hundred pages. The worst part? *I knew she was right.*

As I stared at her review, I had three choices: 1) Wallow in despair, deciding the book was worthless and no one in their right mind would like it; 2) Ignore her advice and hope it was "good enough;" or 3) Do the hard work to bring it up to the standard the story deserved.

I'm not gonna lie, options one and two were *miiiighty* tempting.

It took weeks and weeks of editing, but I rewrote nearly every sentence in the book, using more colorful descriptions, active verbs, and punchier dialogue. And you know what? The new version was worlds better. Not only did it end up securing a publishing deal, *A Gentle Tyranny* even went on to be nominated for a prestigious award.

In life, you're going to face criticism and critique. When you do, you too will have three choices. You can 1) Beat yourself up, believing you're a loser who will never amount to anything; 2) Decide the critic has it wrong (or has it out for you); or 3) Dig deep and do the hard work to make changes. Option three takes serious courage, but I know you're up for it. I can't promise the process will be painless, but if you'll let critique inspire instead of crush you, God can use it to help you become your best self.

Time to Shine

One of the most difficult parts of critique or criticism is knowing whether you should listen to it. Should you view it as someone being mean and let it roll off your back, or as feedback you can use to become a better version of yourself? To tell the difference:

- First, take a look at the critic. Are they someone you can trust? Do they have a reason to lie to you?
- Then ask yourself whether their critique is something you

have the power to change. For example, you can become a better friend, get to places on time, and stop gossiping, but you can't change certain physical characteristics or your core personality. Make sense?

The next time you get criticism from someone, take a moment to evaluate which kind it is, then make changes where you should.

Tip #59

Why so serious? Dance like nobody's watching.

I once joined a Zumba class. If you've never heard of it, Zumba combines rhythmic, dance-your-heinie-off Latin music with high-intensity aerobics to make you sweat profusely while testing every ounce of coordination. Yeah, fun. I've always wished I had the moves of a certain Latina pop star, but alas, my dance floor IQ more closely resembles an injured antelope running for its life. It's not pretty.

When I showed up for class that night, my first instinct was to feel completely self-conscious. Spandex does that. So does a lack of coordination. *What if I can't get the right swing in my hips? What if I get too much swing in my hips? What if I can't keep up or revert to my injured antelope-ish moves?* Fear made me want to turn around and head back to the car.

I scanned the room to see if anyone else looked anxious about what would soon transpire. A middle-aged woman with graying hair caught my attention. She didn't exactly give la vida loca vibes, if you know what I mean. Still, she looked genuinely excited to be there. Tugging her hair into a ponytail, she then pulled something out of her gym bag: a sheer, purple scarf covered in silver discs that jingled like a tambourine when it moved and sparkled in the room's fluorescent lights. It's possible she may have stolen it from a Babylonian belly dancer—can't be certain. I watched as she tied it around her waist and gave her hips a lil' shake to test out the sound. Seriously.

Here I was worried about attracting attention, and this lady was so comfortable in her own skin that she was prepared to stand *way* out from the crowd just to have a little extra fun. I couldn't help but smile. What was my problem? I could either spend the next hour stressed about what others would think of me, getting it all right and blending in, or I could just be me—semi-coordinated, Salsa-music-loving Jessie—and enjoy the evening.

Our instructor, Coco, took the platform. She cranked up the beat, and I shook the insecurities free from my rusty, rhythm-challenged hips. Did I transform into a *Dancing with the Stars* contender? Hardly. But I tell you what, I had a *really* good time. (So did the lone guy in the group, by the way. Bless his brave soul.)

Sometimes you just have to dance like nobody's watching. We can get so hung up on our image and the million things we wish we could change about ourselves that we end up suffocating our personality, talent, and zest for life. That's why I love the way Eugene Peterson paraphrases Romans 12:4–6 in *The Message*:

> Since we find ourselves fashioned into all these excellently formed and marvelously functioning parts in Christ's body, let's just go ahead and be what we were made to be, without enviously or pridefully comparing ourselves with each other, or trying to be something we aren't.

Let's go ahead and be what we were made to be. Yes!

Obviously, that's not a green light to live however we want. After all, we're "made to be" image-bearers of our King. We squeeze the best out of life when we glorify and enjoy Him. But in order to do that, it sure does help when we break free from all those insecurities we've let define us.

Be you. Life is too short to worry what others will think or to give your insecurities full volume in your head. Instead, laugh—really laugh—at things you find funny. Actually talk to that girl you find slightly intimidating. Take risks, enjoy your quirks, and live fully. Dance your way through life, bringing joy and light to the people around you too. A jingly scarf is optional.

Time to Shine

- Have you ever let insecurities keep you from doing something that might have been a lot of fun?
- If you already live a pretty carefree life, what advice would you give someone who has trouble being herself?

Tips About Life Skills

You could think of life skills as a set of tools that will help you build a great life. They help you with things like solving problems, coping with stress, and making decisions. With the right tools, you'll excel—no matter what challenges life throws at you.

Tip #60

Manage your time like you own it or overwhelm will own you.

Once upon a time there lived a knight who possessed a large quantity of treasure, given by the king to reward his heroic deeds. To protect this treasure from thieves, the knight piled his gold, jewels, and sundry valuables in a large cave.

By and by, the knight encountered a traveling merchant selling wares. After purchasing three candles, two tunics, and a trinket promised to ward off plague, the knight noticed a small dragon napping at the merchant's feet.

What fortune! thought the knight. *A dragon could guard my treasure. Then I could return to more important business, like rescuing fair damsels and ousting troublesome ogres.*

"How much for your dragon?" inquired the knight.

The merchant eyed the knight closely. "I will sell you my dragon," he said, *"if* you can manage him."

The brave knight examined the small dragon, no bigger than a goat. "I've rescued fair damsels and ousted troublesome ogres. This small creature is no match for my strength." And it wasn't. The knight had little trouble catching the dragon or chaining him to the entrance of his cave.

With his treasure secured, the knight accepted a commission from the king for a very dangerous, very long, very lucrative quest. Two years passed before the knight returned, weary and injured, with three chests of gold for his troubles.

But when he neared the cave entrance, a ferocious dragon

guarded the opening. A dragon so enormous, so menacing, that even the brave knight didn't dare pass by for fear of his life.

The following summer, the traveling merchant returned to the village. When the knight spotted the man, his anger boiled over.

"The dragon you sold me keeps me from my treasure! It has become a menace. Take him back and I will reward you handsomely."

The merchant's brow furrowed. "If you had taken time to train the dragon when it was young, it would serve you now. But if it has become your master, there is nothing I can do."

When I ask girls, "What's the hardest part of being a teen today?" one of the first responses is always, "Pressure—so much pressure." One of the biggest pressure points? Having more things to do in a day than are humanly possible to get done.

I get it. You've got a ton to do, some of which you've chosen and some that isn't optional. You've got school, sports, youth group, clubs, family time—and let's not forget the importance of keeping up with your friends (in person and online). Maybe sometimes you feel like an enormous dragon is keeping you from the things you want most.

Here's the deal: If you manage your schedule first, it will serve you. Otherwise overwhelm will rob you of the treasure of your time. *Or* time will slip by without you taking advantage of it.

How you guard and manage your time isn't as important as making it a priority. For me? I've learned to keep a calendar and a daily to-do list, to set reminders for important stuff, and to make peace with the uncomfortable prospect of saying *no* so I can give my best *yes* to the things that matter most. I'm not gonna lie, some days I want to tear up my lists and do nothing; other days I long to live in the moment and say yes to all the things! But I've found that telling my schedule what to do instead of the other way around protects the margin I need to live well.

Is a hectic schedule running and ruining your life? Or do you find yourself wasting a lot of time on stuff that doesn't ultimately matter? Either way, if you choose to manage your schedule, it will in turn protect the treasure of your time.

Time to Shine

Circle the following schedule hacks that would serve you this week:

Keep a to-do list

Set reminders for important tasks (including self-care)

Set screen time limits and disable notifications for
    distracting apps

Do the hardest thing first

Keep a consistent bedtime (tiredness makes us lethargic)

Put times for fun and rest on your schedule

Make space by bowing out of some optional activities

Tip #61

Don't trust your memories to your memory. Keep a journal.

"One of the funniest stories about Jess…"

My friend Dani leaned forward with a big, infectious grin—a sure sign a good story was coming. Having been friends since we were seventeen, I've come to appreciate Dani's knack for spinning a side-splitting tale. Our senior year of high school, we met at winter camp, on opposing teams in a heated game of broom hockey. Competitive rivals on the ice rink, we bonded afterward at the snack shack as she regaled us all with a recap of the bruises we gave each other in the matchup. The rest is history, and we have a lot of it. From missions trips to backwoods off-roading, raising kids to navigating tragedy, we both have more than a few stories about the other.

This particular afternoon, I had recently moved to the town she called home, and she was kind enough to invite me to lunch with a group of her friends to make some introductions. I cocked an eyebrow as she launched into the tale…

"So Jess is driving us down this crazy dirt road—literally the middle of nowhere, up in the mountains. We're bumping along, when all of a sudden, we hear a *clang* and the engine gets really loud. So we stop the car, and her tail pipe thing has just fallen right off. And I'm like, 'We're going to DIE in the wilderness!'" (Note: Dani's flair for dramatic exaggeration in storytelling is unmatched and I love her for it. Let's continue.) "So Jess rummages around in the car and finds a roll of duct tape. And she just duct tapes that thing right back on—like MacGyver—and we keep driving!"

I laughed with the rest of the table and nodded knowingly, as if I totally remembered said off-road misfortune. But the truth is, I had completely forgotten about that stupid muffler and its penchant for falling off my parents' car until Dani retold the story.

At the time—when we were young and having adventures on the regular—I never imagined I'd forget something so hilariously random. But a few decades of new memories had pushed it out.

What I do remember about that season of life, in near-perfect clarity, was the time I drove my friends all the way to Ensenada, Mexico, in my mom's white Nissan Maxima, without a map *or* any idea of where we were going to stay. I can picture the lakefront where I spent half the summer of my sixteenth year having picnics during my boyfriend's lunch break. And I *cannot* forget the time I had to pee out of a second story window in the middle of the night on a remote South Pacific island (a tale for another time).

I remember those things because I wrote them down.

A journal captures memories you think you'll never forget, but in ten years probably will. Down the road of life, there will be times when you'll need to remember who you were, what you did, and how far you've come.

A journal also helps you figure out what you think. Process how you feel. Somehow the act of scribbling words on paper acts like a Marauder's Map, revealing where you are in relation to other people, showing you what you're looking for or where you've made a wrong turn.

Show me someone with a rich inner life, and I bet they have a box of dusty journals in their closet (or stacks of poems, song lyrics, or other written musings).

I know you're busy. You don't have to write down every single detail every day of your life. Take some pressure off! Try journaling once a week or once a month. If that's still too much, keep a once-a-year birthday journal. And it doesn't have to be long, either. Sure, you can spill pages of your guts, but if you're not a big writer, simply jot down a sentence or two about the things you hope you don't forget someday. Because if you don't write them down, those memories you think you'll never forget will likely get left in the dust, like a loose tailpipe on a bumpy dirt road.

Time to Shine

Write a journal entry. If you're not sure where to start, you could talk about:

- something or someone you're grateful for today.
- a recent time when God showed up, picked you up, upped the ante, or nudged you to step up.
- a prayer (don't forget to record the answer when it comes!).

Tip #62

Smile. Confidence will take you places.

I'm a sucker for making babies smile. I unabashedly admit this quirk. If there's a toddler in a cart at the checkout line, I'm the weird lady playing peekaboo until I crack through the stranger danger and tug a shy grin from their chubby cheeks. I'm inclined to believe Peter Pan: "You see, Wendy, when the first baby laughed for the first time, its laugh broke into a thousand pieces, and they all went skipping about, and that was the beginning of fairies."[1] I'm just trying to keep the fairies coming, y'all.

Last weekend I visited my extended family in New York. Lucky for me, my nine-month-old nephew was happy to oblige my obsession. At the breakfast table, on the subway, in a stroller—I'd barely have to make eye contact and smile at him and he'd erupt into the most adorable, full-face, one-tooth grin imaginable. I could not handle the cuteness. Over the course of three days, I think we populated an entire fairy village with his delicious giggles.

On the plane ride home, as I suffered through cute nephew withdrawal, I had an epiphany in seat 10F. Babies don't hide their emotions—their reactions come pure and unfiltered. In order for my nephew to smile at me, he must have felt genuine joy, connection, trust. Why would he have felt that way? After all, I had only just met him. I didn't look much like the others in his family. I didn't slip him an extra teething cracker or anything. No, his response

---

1. J.M. Barrie, "Chapter 3: Come Away, Come Away!," *Peter Pan* Lit2Go Edition (1911). https://etc.usf.edu/lit2go/86/peter-pan/1537/chapter-3-come-away-come-away/, accessed October 11, 2023.

was based solely on *my* facial expressions: my smile, eye contact, and general warmth. He trusted me, wanted to be near me, because I engaged him with my face.

Turns out, we don't lose our tendency to read faces when we grow up. Adults, just like babies, are drawn to people who appear confident, look them in the eyes, and, above all, smile. We trust these people and prefer to be near them because they make us feel safe.

During my layover in Dallas, I tested the theory. As I wove through oncoming travelers on my way to the next gate, I challenged myself to make eye contact with each person I passed and smile a little. Not like a Joker grin or anything—just a positive little upturn, a pleasant expression. Surprised by the findings, I tried it again as I boarded the next plane, and the following day at the grocery store. The results held consistent: people responded positively every single time. Sometimes they gave me a smile of their own, sometimes a kind word. Twice, I was rewarded with a door held open for me, and once with a complimentary sparkling water.

Man, smiling can take you places!

I suppose we view smiling people as more confident because it does, in fact, take confidence to smile. If you don't *feel* confident yet, that's okay. Keep working at it. You've probably heard the old saying, "Fake it 'til you make it." I think you'll find it proves true here.

Use the beautiful smile God gave you to spread a little more joy and light in the world. I promise, it'll make your life brighter. And for heaven's sake, if you see a baby, please make all manner of silly faces in my honor. Peter Pan would agree: Neverland could use more fairies.

Time to Shine

Try your own smile experiment. For the next twenty-four hours, practice making eye contact and smiling at the people you talk to or pass by. Whether at fellow students, the clerk at the drive-through, or your own family members, see what a pleasant expression can do, for you *and* for them. Record your findings here or in your journal.

Tip #63

A heavy pack will only weigh you down. Travel light.

Like most American teenagers, I had more clothes than I could wear in a week, shelves lined with knickknacks, drawers of items I hadn't looked at since fifth grade, and a bathroom full of half-used hygiene products. Compared to the people in our community, we weren't considered wealthy. In fact, we were usually stretched pretty thin. Still, I didn't realize how much stuff I had until I left it all to follow God across the world.

The summer after my freshman year of high school, I signed up for a two-month trip with Teen Missions International. I got assigned to Team Fiji. (Yes, suffering for Jesus on a tropical island would be rough, but someone had to do it.) Before we flew overseas, we had to attend a two-week boot camp, where they gave us a military-issue duffel bag and a thirty-pound weight limit for our stuff. We had a few hours to make sure whatever we wanted to take would fit inside.

Now, I didn't think I had brought that much stuff. Just the essentials. But one look at that bag and I knew I'd have to cut my "essentials" in half. *At least.* Our leader pointed to a huge container labeled "missionary barrel" where we could donate anything that didn't fit. Clearly, they were used to overpacking teenagers.

It took me two hours and three trips to the scale to whittle my stuff down to the size and weight limits. In the end, my donations included three pairs of pants, half my makeup, a few shirts, a third of my clothespins, two cans of shaving cream, an extra blanket, a bottle each of shampoo and conditioner, extra batteries, and a travel fan.

The crazy thing is, I didn't miss any of it. In fact, once we had to *carry* those duffel bags through airports and lug them onto ferries, I lightened it even more. It blew my mind that everything I needed for two months could fit in such a small space. Why did I have so much back home? My room was stuffed with stuff.

The Fijians' simple lifestyle made a huge impact on me. They had less compared to my hometown, yet they were full of more joy, Jesus's love, and hospitality. They taught me an important paradox: sometimes the less you have, the happier you'll feel.

I returned home to America and slowly assimilated back into my culture. In time, I could visit the mall again without the materialism bringing me to actual tears. The lesson, though, has stuck. Excess stuff will weigh us down. That's true when traveling, and even more so in life. Because everything I own costs me something, whether money, space, or even the mental energy it takes to deal with it all.

What if we adopted more of a minimalist mindset? What would it look like to fight the desire to own more and more (and more)? What could we gain if we cut back on how much we own and focused on the simple basics instead? I'd wager we'd have about half the styling products, a third of the shoes, hardly any junk drawers, and three times as much space! Best of all, by cutting back, we'd be free to enjoy what we have.

If you're on board with traveling light in life but having trouble deciding what essentials to keep, you could ask yourself:

- Have I used this in a year?
- Does it bring me joy?

- If I lost it in a fire, would I really miss it?
- When I'm twenty-five, will I be glad I still have this?

If the answer is yes, then keep and enjoy it! If no, then let it go with equal joy. Because the lighter you pack in life, the farther you'll be able to go.

Time to Shine

One of the hardest parts of traveling light is letting go of sentimental objects. If you know you need to downsize but find it difficult to say goodbye to that oversized birthday card from your eighth-grade crush or the sweater your grandma knit for you that you just can't bring yourself to wear, ask yourself these questions:

- What memory does this item represent?
- Can I separate my feelings from this item?
- Is there a way I could keep the memory without having to keep the item? (Like by taking a photo or journaling about it?)

Tip #64

Tell your tech who's technically boss.

It happened *again*. Despite telling myself over and over and *over* that this Saturday morning would be different. The night before, I had even put my journal and Bible on my nightstand, right under my phone, to make sure I wouldn't give in. But when my phone's alarm jingled at seven a.m. and I tapped the big orange oval to turn it off, the day's notifications had already sprung to life.

My sister posted a new photo? I had to see what mischief my cute nephew was up to. *Adorable, as always.* I hearted the post and typed a quick reply to tell her so. I had the fleeting thought then that I should set my phone down, but my thumb, which knew the drill, subconsciously flicked the screen, just to see who posted the next photo. It was a random person I followed months ago to enter a contest, but they mentioned an author's new book. Her name sounded vaguely familiar. I jumped over to her profile to see why, then scrolled through eighteen months of posts to find out how she knew so-and-so. On and on it went.

A noise in the kitchen finally pulled me out of the trance. My family was awake. I glanced at the time. *8:37 a.m.* I had just spent ninety-seven full minutes doing absolutely nothing of value, even though I had *promised* myself I wouldn't get on my stupid phone until I had done my devos. *Ugh!* I'm a pretty disciplined person. Why wasn't my self-control enough?

Something snapped that Saturday morning. I was sick and tired of this cycle. How much more time would I let my tech steal from me?

Let me pause here to say that I'm not anti-technology. I have a slew of devices, which I use to write books, keep in touch, discover fascinating facts, book travel, watch movies, and find my way through traffic. I *enjoy* my screens. I'm grateful for them. If given the chance to go back in time to a world before laptops and cell phones, I'd have to really think about it.

That said, I finally came to realize I'm not, in fact, strong enough to resist app creators' monumental efforts to addict us. Technology itself isn't "bad." But our devices, the apps on them, and the endless content is literally *designed* to hook us. Unless I broke technology's hold on me, tech would keep hijacking my life. It was time to tell my screens who the heck was boss.

With a helpful book to guide me, I used my devices' own screen time settings to put limits on everything. I turned off notifications, reorganized my home screens to minimize temptation, and set up "do not disturb" hours. I ordered an actual, old-fashioned alarm clock so I could put my phone "to bed" in the living room at night. Slowly, I detoxed from the addiction, and let me tell you, I was shocked by how much my brain had atrophied. I had to relearn how to simply focus on something for longer than five minutes. But I can also testify that all the color and wonder and joy in life also returned. It was like a fog lifted from my brain and I remembered how much life there was to live.

Screens aren't going anywhere. Keeping them from overrunning your life, then, is vital if you want to get ahead. If you're not being taught how in school, create your own class. It's that important. Read books that specifically teach you how to recognize manipulation, combat distraction, and keep your brain engaged in the real world. You don't *have to* let tech run the show. You're the boss. Is it time you let your screens know?

Time to Shine

If you're not sure whether you're controlling your tech or your tech is controlling you, ask yourself:

- Am I deciding (ahead of time) how long I want to spend on a game, app, or video platform, and then sticking to it?
- Do I have meaningful, face-to-face relationships?
- Can I go a day without it? *Will* I?
- Is it hard for me to focus on one task for a long time?
- How do I feel before I'm on my device? When I'm on it? Afterward?
- Is my tech keeping me from important things, like:
  - » a good night's sleep
  - » finishing homework
  - » time with God
  - » being bored (which often leads to creativity)
  - » hobbies
  - » talking with my family
- Any other questions you'd add?

Tip #65

We all enjoy likable people. Become one of them.

For a small-town high school, we had a surprisingly above-average yearbook. I guess when you only have one stoplight in a twenty-mile radius, people get excited about the little things. Plus, the school had only been open for a couple of years, so we made every new tradition into a giant deal.

My senior year, the hype was real. The yearbook team offered various enticements to make sure we each bought a copy of the snazzy, royal blue book titled "3rd times a charm." (We'll pretend the typo adds to said charm.) In addition to the usual sport and club pages, the seniors would have their own spread of individual quotes, a special class photo, and—most exciting of all—a bunch of "most likely to" awards.

That last one was the big sell for us. Eternal notoriety was on the line. It was a chance to go down in history as the class's most likely to succeed, best dancer, or biggest goof-off. We cast our votes for each category and secretly picked the ones we hoped we'd win. I wouldn't have minded being named "most likely to be on the cover of *Sports Illustrated*" or "most likely to star in the upcoming flick *Babewatch, the Movie*." (Yes, that is the exact wording.) "Best listener" or "funniest" wouldn't be bad either. As long as I didn't get tagged as "biggest flirt" or "always late," I was down.

In the end, I did in fact make the page. I might not have been named prettiest, most athletic, or best dressed, but if my peers had to spend an undetermined amount of time marooned on a spit of land in the middle of the ocean with only *one* other person, who would they want to shuck coconuts with? That's right. "Nobody would object to being stranded on a deserted island with Jessica," complete with a photo of me in a cheap Hawaiian shirt and Gilligan hat.

At the time, I was a little disappointed, but it turns out "likability" is a really great life skill. In fact, it might be one of the most important qualities you can develop. Why? Because deep down, most humans are secretly super insecure. So we gravitate toward people who make us feel seen, special, and understood. We're fond of people like that, and we want to be friends with them, work with them, save opportunities for them. When you're likeable, you come out ahead.

I wasn't always island-mate material, you know. There was a time when my own insecurities made me pretty self-focused and uninteresting. But as Jesus began changing my heart in high school, how I interacted with others changed too. I'm proof that it's possible to become more likable. Here are a few tips:

- **SMILE.** Your warmth will put others at ease.
- **GENUINELY CARE.** Pro tip: This can't be faked. Listen, ask good questions, and put aside your phone to show you care.
- **SPEAK WITH YOUR BODY TOO.** Our brains constantly process nonverbal cues, so stand with confidence, open your shoulders, turn toward the person you're speaking with, and make eye contact.
- **ACCEPT EASILY.** When you forgive, overlook flaws, and avoid gossip, you create an atmosphere of acceptance that draws others in.
- **SHINE POSITIVITY.** Optimism is endearing. Look on the bright side and people will look to you.

- **BE TRANSPARENT.** You don't have to share all your secrets, but vulnerability multiplies.
- **BE INCLUSIVE.** If life's a big table, a likable person says there's always room for one more. They make others feel welcome.
- **USE PHYSICAL TOUCH.** Think fist bump, hug, or a friendly touch on the shoulder. Positive, welcomed touch releases oxytocin in our brains (aka, happy hormones), endearing you to others.
- **DON'T TAKE YOURSELF TOO SERIOUSLY.** We all make mistakes. If you can turn yours into a self-deprecating joke, others will feel safer to make mistakes too.

Likeability isn't so much about *becoming* like other people as it is about learning to genuinely *like* other people. You can be more confident and caring without becoming a chameleon. And likeability isn't just for the lucky few born with good looks and outgoing personalities. All of the traits I just listed can be developed. If you commit to working on them, I'm confident unexpected doors will open for you. At the very least, you'll be a better version of yourself, whether or not you're ever stranded on an island with your friends.

Time to Shine

Think about the people you most enjoy being around. Which skills/ qualities from the list above do you see in them? Put a star next to any you want to personally work on.

Tip #66

Clean up the clutter to clear up your mind.

Picture this with me: After a long, stressful day, you get home and head to your room. You need some space to chill and do homework. When you swing open the door, you're greeted with what could be mistaken for news footage of a tornado ripping through suburbia. Clothes cover the floor and half the unmade bed. Last night's dinner dishes, a half-finished craft project, and a stack of books line the dresser. Your favorite chair is hidden by a pile of old assignments and the gym bag you've been meaning to clean out for three weeks. For a split second, you consider cleaning up before starting tonight's homework, but that sounds way overwhelming and you're already exhausted. As you toss the clothes from your bed over to the growing pile on your chair so you can sit down, how do you imagine you'd feel?

Okay, now picture this: After a long, stressful day, you get home and head to your room. You're ready to chill and tackle tonight's homework. When you swing open the door, the space looks clean and bright. Your bed is made, the floor clear, and sunlight reflects on the empty dresser top. You drop your backpack and exhale slowly as you sink into your favorite chair. How do you imagine you'd feel?

I'm guessing you, like me, would take option two in a heartbeat. Our spaces affect us. Clutter adds stress, but clean rooms bring focus and peace, which can inspire greater creativity and a more positive outlook on life.

I don't know anyone who would *prefer* to live in scenario one; it's just that keeping stuff organized 1) takes time and effort, and 2) doesn't usually come naturally. It's a skill we have to learn.

Whether you have a room to yourself or share it with a roommate, live in a tiny apartment or a sprawling estate, I promise it's worth it to learn how to create a space that inspires you.

We've already tackled the first step: Travel light in life (see Tip #63). The fewer things you have, the easier it will be to manage your stuff.

Now it's time to organize what you have. The goal? Give every item a "home," preferably out of sight. If it doesn't have a place, it'll just fill your space. Think about it: if you have too many shoes to fit on your shoe rack, where do you think they're gonna end up? In a pile on the floor of your closet, naturally. If necessary, go back to step one. Then get creative with containers, drawers, baskets, etc., to hide stuff away. Once everything has a place, it'll be way easier to tackle the next step, which is . . .

Actually put things in their places. If you take a few minutes each day to tidy up, you'll rarely get to the tornado-level cleaning job that makes you want to procrastinate indefinitely and costs you an entire Saturday (plus half your sanity) to tackle. Make your bed, put dirty clothes in the hamper, take the dishes to the kitchen. Every day. Build those habits, and soon you won't even have to think about it.

A clean space might seem like a small thing, but it has the power to make a big impact on your mental clarity, helping you achieve the life you ultimately want.

Time to Shine

On a scale of one to ten, how would you rate your organizational skills? If a cleaner space sounds refreshing, set a day to begin downsizing and organizing. Enlist the help of a friend or family member to help keep you on track and encourage you along the way.

Tip #67

You'll fill whatever time you have for a task. Schedule accordingly.

Recently, I had seven hours to write two short columns. Since that was *pa-lenty* of time—more than usual—I figured I'd start by making something special for breakfast. While drinking my smoothie, I unloaded the dishwasher. Responded to two text messages. Deposited an online check. Sat down to write. Got up to go to the bathroom. Poured some tea on the way back to my chair. Stared at the screen for twenty-six minutes. Remembered I needed to start a load of laundry. On my way to the laundry room, I noticed the car was filthy enough to write "Jessie was here" on the rear window. Washing the car simply could not wait. After sudsing it up, I returned to my chair. Wrote the first paragraph. Deleted the first paragraph. Wrote a new paragraph. Researched goal-setting strategies. Got sidetracked by a study that compared twelve ways to hard-boil eggs. (I wish I were making this up.) Made hard-boiled eggs. Eked out a handful more sentences. By mid-afternoon, I was questioning whether I'd ever actually finish.

All told, it took me 5.7 hours to write 605 words. A new record, I think.

Want to guess how long the second article took me to write? I'll tell you. One hour and seven minutes. Want to know why? Because I only had one hour and eight minutes before I had to leave.

Parkinson's law states that work expands to fill the time available for its completion. The more time you have for a task, the longer it will take you to finish.

For example, if you have forty-five minutes to get ready for school in the morning, you'll get ready in forty-five minutes. You could swear there's nothing you could do to get ready faster. But if you accidentally snooze your alarm and wake up ten minutes late, you'll somehow find a way to get your booty out the door in thirty-five. You following?

This principle applies to homework, chores, work, screen time, and more. And the law gets magnified when we have to do something challenging, annoying, or unpleasant. English essay? Yeah, we'll get distracted from our *distractions* rather than buckle down to get that done.

It happens to the best of us. That's why understanding and then using Parkinson's law to your *advantage* is a great life skill to develop. The key is to give yourself reasonable, realistic time frames to get the job done.

Let's take that English essay, for example. You want to give yourself enough time, but not too much. Imagine you get home from school at four thirty. If you sit down at the computer without a plan, you could spend the next five hours repeating your personal version of the ridiculous distractions I detailed earlier, barely finishing by bedtime. *Or* you could take five minutes to think over your task list and stuff you want to do and then schedule out the time you have. It might look something like this:

4:30–5:30: Write English essay

5:30–6:15: Dinner break

6:15–6:45: Finish essay

6:45–7:15: Take a walk

7:15–7:45: Math assignment

7:45–8:15: Hang out with family

8:15–9:00: Shower and get ready for bed

By limiting the amount of time you have for a challenging assignment, you'll actually spend less time completing it, leaving more time for the stuff that brings you life and joy. If you know you don't have time for distractions, you'll be less likely to give in to them.

Parkinson's law still might bite you in the butt sometimes (obviously, I'm not completely immune either!), but the more you practice using it to your advantage, the more productive you'll be with your time. And having free time for the things you love makes life brighter.

Time to Shine

For the next few days, practice being mindful of how much time you spend doing normal tasks. How long does it take you to get ready in the morning, do homework, your chores, etc.? Are you happy with those time frames? Do they need adjustment? If you notice any consistent distractions that eat up your time, schedule a plan to minimize them.

Tip #68

Make a budget, no matter how much you make.

Once upon a time, Fiona's summer job earned her a chunk of change, which she put in the bank like a responsible person. She wanted to buy a car, after all. When she went back to school, though, that money gave her unexpected new freedom. She could use her card to pick up a drink from her favorite smoothie shop on the way to class, buy that cute outfit she saw online, and didn't think twice when her friends invited her to an expensive concert. Why would she say no if she had money in the bank? But at the end of the year, her account was as empty as it had been before. When her parents' neighbor offered to sell her his car at a deep discount, she couldn't afford to buy it.

Sadie's summer job earned her the same income as Fiona's. She deposited each paycheck into her bank account like a responsible person. Since she wanted to buy a car, she knew she'd have to budget her money wisely, so she downloaded an app that helped her keep track of her funds. After designating some money as an offering back to God, she split up the rest into categories like "car savings," "eating out," and "miscellaneous." It was hard not to spend that hard-earned cash when her friends were going to a concert on a Friday night, but she found other ways to treat herself for less. She learned to shop at thrift stores, borrowed a dress for the formal, and made her favorite tea latte at home instead of driving through the coffee shop. At the end of the year, her bank account proved she had managed her money well. And it was worth it! When her parents' neighbor offered to sell her his car at a deep discount, she smiled as she took the keys.

Money itself isn't good or evil, it's just a tool. Dollars represent choices. For example, when you have money, you can choose to go out to eat with it or to buy a homeless person a meal. You can decide to purchase a car or pay for your education. If you want to get your nails done, that's a choice you have, or you could save that money to rent a nicer apartment later. But if you don't consciously decide what you want that money to do for you (and/or for others), you'll likely "choose" to spend it on whatever feels important in the moment (and nothing feels more important than takeout when you're hungry!).

Every successful, money-wise person I know has some type of a budget. I don't think that's a coincidence. A budget helps you choose what to do with your money while you're clear-headed. You can get the big picture, then map out a plan to longer-term goals. And it can help hold you accountable for your impulse purchases. Even if you don't have a lot, you can still be intentional with what you have.

Be wise with the money God trusts you with. If you can learn to manage it well now, the choices you'll have later will multiply— including the choice to be generous with it.

Time to Shine

If you don't already have one, make a budget to keep track of what you make and where you want it to go. If you're still in the occasional-babysitting-money phase of life, you could write out a simple budget on notebook paper, or label three envelopes "tithe," "spend," and "save." Do you have a job or regular allowance? Consider using a budgeting app that will make it easier to keep track of your spending and help you stick to long-term goals. Your bank might offer a free option. I've used several budget systems over the years. My current favorite is You Need a Budget (https://www.ynab.com).

Tip #69

Learn to resist peer pressure, and you'll keep a clear mind (and conscience).

I grabbed a red plastic cup from the table and lifted it to my lips. The tangy-sweet scent of fermented hops reminded me of Dad's favorite beer, Dos Equis. Apart from an occasional taste of his, I had never had a beer myself. In high school, I was known as a good girl—one of those "Jesus Freaks" who shied away from the local parties. In fact, this was the first *real* party I had ever been to. And I was jumping in with both feet.

I had driven the three hours to San Diego State University with two guy friends, Jet and Chad, to watch their buddy Kaleb play in a big rugby match. I had been spending a lot of time with Jet lately. He kept inviting me to do stuff, and since he was a super nice guy and we always had a great time, I kept saying yes. Okay, I was *fairly certain* that Jet had feelings for me, but I wasn't interested in more than friendship. It just sounded like fun to road trip and watch a sport I had never seen, so off the three of us went.

During the rugby match, I learned about the scrum and the difference between a tackle, ruck, and maul. It was a riot. Everything was going great, and then, after the game, I met their friend Kaleb. He was *really* cute. And within five minutes, he was flirting like he was keen to get to know me. If Jet showed any signs of jealousy, I ~~didn't~~ tried *not* to notice.

"You guys should stay for the party tonight," Kaleb said. "It'll be awesome."

Having never been to a college frat party, Chad looked at

Jet, who looked at me. I looked at Kaleb and nodded a little too enthusiastically.

And that's how I ended up at my first and only frat party. As I held that red Solo cup in my hands, music blaring and students dancing, I had no intention whatsoever of getting drunk. Honest. I figured I'd just hold on to it so I wouldn't look out of place. Maybe I'd take a sip now and then. But as Kaleb led us from one building to another, the fizzy liquid in my cup somehow disappeared, right along with my inhibitions.

By the time Kaleb took my arm and led me onto a moonlit balcony, my better sense had floated away and left stars in my eyes. In my slightly inebriated state, the scene felt magical, romantic. With waves crashing in the distance, a handsome rugby player's strong arms pulled me closer. He kissed me. And I kissed back.

When we pulled apart, someone else stood at the balcony entrance, stock-still, like he had been sucker punched on the rugby field. Unmistakable hurt burned in Jet's eyes. I had betrayed his friendship, and his deep feelings for me, with some hot guy I knew nothing about. A guy who was supposed to be his friend.

An hour later, I was lying dizzy on the back seat of Chad's car as we made the drive home. Jet was kind enough to care for me on the way, and made sure I got back to my dorm. But our friendship was never the same. Though I tried to patch things up, he had seen a side of me that was completely incongruent with the girl he had admired.

That night on the balcony remains one of the clearest, most painful memories I have of hurting someone. It's also the reason I'm *really* careful about drinking, smoking, or ingesting *anything* that could take my better sense from me. The lesson came at a high price. I share mine in the hopes that you'll avoid paying one too.

Just because they are socially acceptable doesn't mean

substances like alcohol, marijuana, nicotine, or even caffeine won't cost you something. They alter your cognitive function. Some might say for the better, but an old saying applies here: Nothing is ever free. You might feel great for a bit, but you're only borrowing joy, peace, or energy from tomorrow. You always have to pay it back.

In the book of Proverbs, a king's mom gives her son some advice about keeping a clear mind:

> It is not for kings, Lemuel—it is not for kings to drink wine, not for rulers to crave beer, lest they drink and forget what has been decreed, and deprive all the oppressed of their rights (Proverbs 31:4–5).

As daughters of *the* King—as girls under God's decree to bring justice and goodness to the world on His behalf—the queen mother's wise words apply just as much to you and me. I don't see biblical evidence that drinking or smoking are always sins. Just warnings to treat them *very* carefully. I personally understand why.

Your mind—your thinking, agency, ability to reason and be rational—is easily hijacked. Guard it like your happiness and success depend on it, no matter who's pressuring you.

Time to Shine

- Have you ever thought you had something under control, only to find out later it had control of you?
- What qualities do you think drive people who can say no to peer pressure?
- What practical guardrails do you need to set for yourself to make sure you're always in control of your decision-making?

Tip #70

Wait for a better payout, and the rewards will be sweet.

One of my favorite random videos opens with a single marshmallow resting on a Styrofoam plate on a desk in an otherwise empty room.[1] It appears the marshmallow will soon be interrogated by the sugar police—that's the vibe. Instead, a woman escorts a preschool boy through the door and invites him to take a seat at the desk, inches from the treat.

"Alright, here's the deal," she says. "The marshmallow's for you. You can wait, and I'll give you another one *if you wait*. Or you can eat it now."

The little boy nods in understanding, and the video cuts to other preschool children receiving the same instructions. What follows is a hilarious montage of tiny people trying *very hard* to resist the pillowy sweetness right under their noses. But it's so . . . fluffy. Sweet. Squish-alicious. Is it *really* worth the wait? Some decide not. One girl has half the marshmallow in her mouth before the woman even walks away. Others pick it up and smell it. Squish it between their fingers, set it back down. Kiss it. Pick the tiniest little nibble off the corner, then look around to see if anyone's watching. The strongest stare at it longingly, fingers drumming on the table, or hide their eyes, trying valiantly to resist.

My favorite moment comes three minutes in, when the first boy, who came *so close* to eating it, makes it to the end, and the

---

1. "The Marshmallow Test." Igniter Media. https://www.youtube.com/watch?v=QX _oy9614HQ&t=26s, accessed March 12, 2024.

woman gives him the second promised marshmallow. Exhausted from the willpower it took to wait, but elated at his victory, he shoves *both* into his mouth at once. A sweet reward!

Those preschoolers were faced with an internal battle between present pleasure or greater enjoyment later. Experts call waiting for a better payout "delayed gratification." Why do I share it with you? Because those who learn the skill come out ahead in life.

In fact, the researchers who conducted the original Marshmallow Experiment, published in 1972, followed the kids for decades afterward. They found that over time, the children who were willing to wait for the greater payout excelled in pretty much every area of life. They had lower rates of obesity, scored higher academically, were less likely to abuse alcohol or drugs, and coped better with stress.[2]

If faced with the choice, what would you do? Eat one marshmallow now or wait for two?

Logically, we know waiting for a greater payout makes sense. Waiting doesn't cost you anything but time. The thing is, we'll only wait for the better, later reward if we can measure it. If the woman had told the preschoolers, "You can have the marshmallow now, or you can wait," none of them would have waited. Why would they if they didn't get anything *better* by waiting?

If you want to grow in delayed gratification, get in the habit of naming the better reward. For example:

- I *could* scroll on my phone now—that would be fun—but if I

2. Mischel, W et al. "Delay of gratification in children." *Science* (New York, N.Y.), vol. 244, 4907 (1989): 933-8. doi:10.1126/science.2658056, accessed October 19, 2023. https://pubmed.ncbi.nlm.nih.gov/2658056/.

study instead, I'll be even happier when I get better grades later.

- I *could* watch another episode of this awesome show, but if I turn off the TV, I can get a good night's sleep and have a clearer mind tomorrow.
- I *could* spend my whole paycheck on a new car payment, or I could get a cheaper car and invest the difference so I'll have greater financial independence when I'm older.

Even if you're the type to eat the marshmallow three seconds in, don't give up on yourself. We can all grow in self-discipline over time. Start small. Sacrifice some of your wants today and sweet rewards will await you later. I promise your effort will be worth it. How do I know? Because delayed gratification is at the heart of living your best, brightest life. Easy says go with the flow. Greatness takes vision, sacrifice, and intentionality. There will be days you wonder if the sacrifices are worth it. But when you name the reward—in this case, the life you're truly after—you'll be more likely to stay the course today and enjoy double the blessings tomorrow.

Time to Shine

If you want to get better at waiting for a bigger payout, name some rewards specific to your life. I'll help guide the first few, then you can fill in the blanks with some of your own:

WHAT I WANT TO DO NOW	ALTERNATIVE	REWARD
Get physical with my boyfriend	Stick to my boundaries	Healthier, guilt-free relationship
Eat a bowl of ice cream	Make a fruit smoothie	Clearer skin, healthier body
Skip the gym	Work out	Stronger body, better mood

Of Monsters and Courage
(One Last Story)

I touched poison oak today.

Before we get into that, let me tell you one more story. A children's story.

When I was a preschooler, I loved to read *The Monster at the End of this Book*. In it, Sesame Street's "loveable, furry old Grover" notices that the title page says there's—wait for it—a monster at the end of the book. Completely freaked, he begs the reader not to turn any pages, to prevent a run-in with what he imagines will be a terrifying creature. When the reader disobeys, turning page after page, Grover panics. He tries tying the pages together with rope, then builds a brick wall on another. He begs the reader to reconsider. Much to Grover's dismay, the reader presses on and on, too strong for his antics. Pages are torn, walls toppled, and wood boards ripped apart, sending the furry blue narrator into a frenzy of fear. Doesn't the reader understand that there is a *monster* at the end of the book? Why chance going any farther? Quitting now would be the safe bet.

But, after all his fussing, when we finally get to the last page, it turns out that he's the only one there. Lovable, furry old Grover *was* the monster at the end of the book.

Since writing the introduction to *Your Brightest Life*, I've felt a bit like Grover. Before I finished these pages, I knew I'd have to answer a critical question: *Did Jim's crazy idea work?* I'd actually have to touch Pacific poison oak to see whether I had, in fact, built up an immunity. Each chapter I wrote got me closer to the end of the book, and some days I dragged my feet like there was a monster waiting for me. Because, well, what if there was? Like, a really itchy one? I had no guarantee this was going to work.

Despite my best stalling tactics, I eventually finished tip number seventy. It was time to turn the final page.

Adrenaline surged as I browsed a clearing for a glistening poison oak leaf. I was fairly confident in Jim's advice—I hadn't died from eating it all these months. Still, my stomach did flips as I touched one of the leaves to my skin, covered the spot with a bandage, and waited.

Day one, nothing. Days two and three, felt great. On day six, three tiny bumps developed, started itching a bit. It took everything in me not to panic, to trust the process. Merciful heavens, they never got bigger, and by day thirteen, even those small spots were healing. After two weeks post-touch, I let out a sigh of relief and announced to my family and friends that Jim's crazy idea had worked.

When we hear advice that resonates deep in our soul, it's easy to nod in agreement. We might even repeat that advice to someone else we think needs to hear it. But unless we actually take a risk and try it out, we'll never know if it works. And that often involves facing our fears.

I've shared some of the best advice I know about living a bright, fulfilling, hope-filled life. If these tips resonated with you, don't stop there. Put them to the test. See how they work out for you.

I'll be honest, there's an element of risk. I can't promise following these tips will make your life rainbows and lollipops. You'll
still face challenges you didn't see coming, and setbacks that hurt
deeply. As long as you know that going in, you'll be free to see your
whole life as one big learning experience. A chance to grow, fail, and
get back up again. Again and again.

Whatever you do, don't let fear stop you. After all, like Grover
learned, fear of the thing is almost always worse than the thing
itself. So keep turning those pages.

Bring God glory by living fully alive. Be brave, curious, and
wise. Value the people in your life and work at your relationships.
Open your heart to love and adventure, even if that also opens you
to loss and risk. Never stop learning, growing, and becoming. God
loves you and has good plans for you. No matter what comes your
way, remember: You only get one life. So make it your brightest.

Want to learn more about life, love, and God with me?

For Help Navigating Relationships

Get a crash course in romance dos and don'ts with *Crushed: Why Guys Don't Have to Make or Break You*

If You're Fighting a Secret Sin

Ditch shame and start healing in *Unashamed: Overcoming the Sins No Girl Wants to Talk About*

If You Can't See Your Own Beauty

Discover your true worth in *Backwards Beauty: How to Feel Ugly in 10 Simple Steps*

When Your Family Drives You Crazy

Get practical tips for the drama in *Family: How to Love Yours (And Help Them Like You Back)*

And visit **LifeLoveandGod.com** for more, including hundreds of posts where I answer questions from girls like you!

Acknowledgments

If I were to write a complete "Bright Side List" about the making of this book, I'd need another twenty pages! Will you at least indulge me in this abbreviated version?

The journey from idea to finished copy has had God's fingerprints all over it, and He gifted me with an incredible team of people who have believed in this vision as much as I do. First on that list, a huge thanks to my agent (and all-around great human) Andrew Wolgemuth, for being willing to take yet another chance with me. Cheers to the history, and to the future, my friend!

My number one partner in love and crime, Paul Daniel: half of these stories exist because my story includes the adventure of you. I'm so grateful for your endless support, much-needed humor, and unmatched web and video skills. We make a good team.

God may have asked me to write this book, but He chose the Zonderkidz team to champion it, and I couldn't have asked for a better partnership. Megan Dobson, from day one your passion for this project was contagious, and your expertise has taken the message to the next level. Working with you has been a true delight. Jacque Alberta, thanks for polishing her up proper (I hereby take 100 percent responsibility for any remaining traces of improper tenses and made-up words). Kudos to Micah Kandros for the beautiful cover. Abby Van Wormer, Sara Merritt, and Jessica Westra, thank you for working behind the scenes to bring *Your Brightest Life* into the spotlight.

A huge and heartfelt thanks to my amazing early readers Bella Craig, Callie Hughes Farmer, Christy Olmstead, Ellie Heilig, Jocelyn Olmstead, Logan Minassian, LoreLai Davis, and Ryan Minassian. You girls are absolutely amazing, and your feedback made this a better book!

A special shoutout to Converse the cat, whose editorial "help," though a bit pushy at times, brought much inspiration. And to his people for use of their idyllic sunroom, where most of these pages were penned.

Finally, I'm grateful for YOU! Thank you for choosing to spend your time with me and trusting me to speak into your journey. I don't take that honor lightly. Also, you now know a lot of embarrassing things about me, which in my mind makes us friends. So if we get the chance to meet in person, give me a big hug, will ya?